Brothers Have Talent, Too

by Melisa Torres

Illustrated by Daniel Ramos and Carrie Arnold

To Logan and Christopher,
It is a joy watching you grow and develop your
talents. You are amazing boys!
Love,
Mom

Chapter 1

Cast to Horizontal on Bars

"Alexis, what is this flyer?" my mom asks holding up a piece of blue paper that says Winter Wonderland Talent Show.

"It's for a talent show," I say.

"Are you going to do it?" she asks, her blue eyes sparkling with delight.

I know she is dying for me to participate. I

decide to mess with her a little. "Maybe. I'm not sure. What talents do I have?"

She puts down the paper and starts rummaging through my brothers' back packs. "Well, I know what I would do if I were you, Baby Girl," she says, pulling out more papers and skimming them.

My mom calls me Baby Girl because I'm her fifth child and only girl. She says I will always be her baby. I don't really mind. I've noticed, though, since I started third grade she has stopped calling me Baby Girl in public.

"Boys!" she yells upstairs, "Come down here for Table Time!" A thunder of footsteps echo down the stairs as the boys come running.

"How come she's not at Table Time?" Ethan asks, as he passes me sitting at the kitchen counter.

"She's still finishing her snack. She eats like a lady, unlike you crazies," my mom teases.

I pick up my apple slice and slowly eat it while I listen to my mom settle the boys in at the table. Table Time in our house means we all sit at the dining room table and do our homework. We don't eat at the dining table all week because it's a huge mess of books, homework, papers, pencils, crayons, backpacks, and glue. It stays like this all week. But on Sundays my mom clears it off so we can have a big family dinner after church.

I have four brothers: Josh, William, Ethan and Drew. My oldest brother, Josh, is at basketball practice while the other three are at Table Time with my mom.

"Andrew, when is this book report due?" my mom asks Drew.

"Friday, I think."

"Good thing you've been reading *Adeline Falling Star*, you can use that," she decides.

"Alexis! You should be done by now. No more stalling." I reluctantly slide off my stool and head toward the dining room. I bet Josh never got rushed during his after school snack when he was a third grader.

As I get to the dining room I see William, Ethan, and Drew bent over their homework. My mom has my spot ready with my spelling words out.

"Let's see, when are the talent show tryouts?" My mom picks up the blue paper again from the pile she has brought in from the kitchen.

"Talent Show?" Drew asks, looking up.

"There's a talent show at Mountain View. You should do it, too," my mom says to Drew.

"What would I do?" Drew asks.

"What about tumbling to music?" my mom asks. Drew is my only brother that isn't into basketball or baseball. He does gymnastics like me.

"No thanks, boys don't tumble to music."

"They might in talent shows," she says.

"That's something for Alexis to do," he says, and goes back to his homework.

"Do you want to do it, Baby Girl? I could help you put something together," my mom says. I can tell she really wants me to do the talent show.

When my teacher announced the talent show in class I was excited. I thought Drew would do it with me. He can tumble so well and it would be so cool if we did the show together. I glance up at my mom, I know she is expecting an answer.

"I don't want to do it by myself," I confess. "Are you sure you don't want to do it, Drew?" I ask my brother. He looks up and shakes his head no.

"Male gymnasts don't perform to music," he insists.

"Maybe my teammates will do it with me?"

"What a great idea!" my mom exclaims, "You can ask them at practice today."

"Can they come over on Saturday to make something up?" I'm getting excited about this. Paige could create the dance and Trista could do her back flip. Everyone at school would see how cool it is to be a gymnast.

"You have the Team Banquet and sleepover

this Friday. Why don't you just make up something at the sleepover?"

"The banquet is this Friday? Finally!" I am so excited for the end of season banquet.

"I know it feels like you've been waiting forever, but it's only January and your season ended in November. December is a hard month to do anything. I'm sure Katie and James were just busy. Anyway, better late than never," Mom says, walking over to her place at the table. She sits down and picks up her book to read while we work.

"Will we get trophies like the boys do after their baseball and basketball season?" I ask.

"I'm not sure, but probably not. My guess is each of you will be recognized in some way. But gymnastics isn't really a sport that gives participation trophies. You get medals and ribbons all season."

"What do you mean recognized in some way?" Drew asks.

"When I was a kid we could get Most

Improved and MVP trophies. But I'm not sure if Katie will do that or give out any awards. We have to just wait and see," she says, looking down at her book.

"What's MVP?" I ask.

"Most Valuable Player. Haven't you been to all the same baseball banquets I've been to?" Drew asks.

"Yeah, but I never paid attention. They're boring."

"Hey!" Ethan looks up from his work, "It's not as if going to a gymnastics meet is a picnic. The same stupid music over and over again is nightmare!"

"At least no one is spitting!" I yell.

"Hey, you two," my mom raises her voice and we immediately stop shouting. We don't want to be in here longer than we have to be. She has extra workbooks and worksheets for us to do if we misbehave. We quiet down and go back to our homework.

I stare at my spelling words while I think about

the banquet. Would I be MVP? No, Marissa would probably get that. Most Improved That would probably go to Trista. Did I do anything special this season? What about Paige and Savannah? What would James give them? I still really hope we all get trophies.

After the banquet when we are at the sleepover we can make up the best gymnastics and dance routine ever. We'll perform it at my school and my mom will be so proud.

"Alexis," I look up to see my mom is staring at me. "Are you ready for me to give you a spelling test?" she asks.

"Yes," I say. It's lucky that I'm good at spelling. She'll think I was studying instead of day dreaming about trophies and talent shows.

Chapter 2

Tap Swings on Bars

"There's a talent show at my school and I was thinking we could do a gymnastics and dance routine. Would you guys want to do that with me?" I ask my teammates, Trista, Savannah, and Marissa.

"I'm in. I'd love to Lex," I smile, I figured Trista would want to do the talent show.

"What would we do exactly?" Marissa asks.

"A dance routine or something with gymnastics in it," I answer. At least that's what my mom said we should do.

"Hi, guys," Paige says, walking up to us. We are at the cubbies at Perfect Balance Gymnastics Academy putting our shoes and jackets away before practice begins. We leave our leggings on because it is cold in the gym today.

"Why do you all look so serious?"

"Alexis wants us to do a talent show with her at her school," Savannah supplies.

"Oooh, that sounds fun," Paige says, then they all start talking at once with ideas and opinions about what song to use, how to incorporate gymnastics, and who should do what. Before I can grab onto any one idea our coach, James, pokes his head out of the office door that connects to the lobby. He tells us to run around the floor ten times to warm up then disappears back to the office.

We walk through the glass doors into the

training area and over to floor. Paige turns to me, "Let's figure it out at PNO this week." She is referring to Parents' Night Out. Parents' Night Out is at Perfect Balance every Friday night. We can play in the gym and play on the equipment in a way we are not allowed to during practice. We eat pizza, play games, and build forts with the mats. Our parents like it because they get to go out to dinner. Everyone loves PNO, except sometimes James. He complains about having to work late on those nights.

"Isn't our team sleepover this week?" Trista asks.

"Oh yeah," Paige turns to me as we start running around the edge of the floor, "we'll have plenty of time at the sleepover to come up with something."

James comes out of the office into the training area just as we are on our last lap. "Ten tuck jumps," he instructs. I have more questions for Paige but I'm going to have to wait.

We do our tuck jumps, split jumps, and

straddle jumps. Then we sit down to do some light stretching. That's when the talking begins again.

"James, can we compete this spring?" Trista asks as soon as we sit in our splits. "I went to a Level 7 meet over the weekend and I was sitting next to some Level 3 girls from Salt Lake Gymnastics and they said there is a spring and fall season for compulsories," she explains. I can tell Trista has been dying to ask James this question all weekend.

"I am aware of that Trista and no. At PBGA we compete one compulsories season, the fall season," he answers.

"But why?" she asks.

"Because doing routines every day during season takes time away from learning new skills. At PBGA we teach you your new skills in the spring rather than competing," he explains.

"Then how do other gyms do both?" she asks.

"They train more hours," he says simply.

"Can we train more hours?" Trista asks.

"Not at PBGA," he says. "Make sure to stretch

your wrists and let's start on bars," he says to the group.

"Why?" Trista presses.

James stops to look at Trista and finally says, "Why do you think we're called Perfect Balance Gymnastics Academy?" he asks.

"Because gymnasts have to be perfect and have balance?" She ventures.

At this point we are all standing up ready to go to bars, but we are waiting for James' answer.

"That's part of it. The other part is balance in life. Katie named her gym Perfect Balance Gymnastic Academy because she liked the idea of teaching gymnasts balance in life. Training 15 hours a week as a Level 4 is, in her opinion, not balance. Those kids do not have time for other hobbies."

He looks at us to make sure we are all listening. "Gymnastics is wonderful for kids, but you still need to be a kid. Play with friends, have hobbies and do things with your families. Two seasons would be more work," he says.

"But what if we don't want other hobbies? Don't you think with two seasons we could move up the levels faster?" Trista asks.

"Probably, but what's the rush? What grade are you in? Fourth?" he asks.

"Third," she answers.

"Trista, you have nine years to move up seven more levels. What's the rush?" he asks.

Trista is quiet, she is finally out of questions. James sees this and says, "Put your pants away, time for bars."

Nine years to move up seven more levels. If I want to do gymnastics in college, like my mom, I must become a Level 10. We have a certain amount of time to get to Level 10? I wonder if my mom knows this. I wonder if I'm ahead or behind schedule. I'll have to ask her. My mind is now moving faster than Trista's as I walk to bars. How old was my mom when she was a Level 3? Why doesn't my mom have me at Salt Lake Gymnastics if she wants me to compete in college?

"Want to share a bar, Lex?" Carmen asks me, shaking me out of my thoughts. Carmen is Trista's friend from Level 2. She has been working out with us since our competition season ended.

"Sure." I say jumping to a support.

Chapter 3

Front Handspring on Vault

I'm waiting in the lobby of PBGA watching
the snow coming down in big fat snowflakes.
January is cold in Snowcap Canyon. I see my
mom's car turn into the parking lot and I yell over
to Drew who is goofing around with his
teammate Aaron, "Mom's here!"

"Gotta go bro. See you tomorrow," Drew says

to Aaron and trots over to me. I shove on my knit hat and gloves. Drew is hopping on one foot trying to pull on his second boot.

"You should have been ready. She hates to wait," I say to him.

"I am ready," he says as he finishes pulling on his boots. He looks up and gives me a lopsided grin. We walk out the door as she pulls up.

"Hi, how was practice?" she asks, as we climb into the car.

"Good, we got to vault over the table today," I answer.

"I bet that's hard," she says.

"Didn't you do it?" I ask her, confused. My mom was a Level 10 gymnast and she competed for BYU (Brigham Young University), so I'm used to her knowing all my skills and remembering how she learned them.

"Back then vault was not a vaulting table. It was a horse. It was shaped like Andrew's Pommel Horse, without the pommels."

"That's weird," Drew says.

My mom laughs, "That's just how it was. But It was easier to get over in a handspring vault than the new table," she explains.

"Why would they make it harder?" I ask.

"I think it's harder for you to learn the handspring as a small person, but when you get to the higher levels and you have more surface area to connect with the table, I imagine it will be easier than the horse. I think it was changed for safety on the high level vaults, like the Yurchenko," she says.

"What's a Yurchenko?" I ask.

"You've seen it. It's a round off entry onto the board and back handspring onto the table," she explains. Oh yeah, I've seen kids in the gym from the higher levels do that vault, I just never knew the name. Yurchenko.

"What did you work on tonight Andrew?" My mom asks.

"Level 5 stuff," he says.

The car is quiet for a moment and I'm thinking about Salt Lake Gymnastics and how they get to compete this spring. I look over at Drew and he is rummaging through his gym bag. Any chance he gets he plugs in his mp3 player and ear buds and is listening to music.

"Mom?"

"Hmm?" she says absently.

"Why do you have us at a gym that doesn't train as much as other gyms?" I ask.

"How do you know how much other gyms train?" she asks.

"Trista met some girls from Salt Lake Gymnastics and they get to do gymnastics for more hours and they get to compete this spring."

"Maybe Trista was exaggerating about how much they work out," Drew comments and with that he puts in his ear buds, leans back his seat, and stacks his hands behind his head.

My mom sighs, "Baby girl, there is more to life than gymnastics," she says.

"There wasn't for you," I point out.

"No, there wasn't and sometimes I'm sad I didn't get to do other things."

"What else would you have done?"

"I'm not sure, dance maybe, or cheer, or art, or maybe just more time to hang out with friends. I want you to have more balance than I had."

"That's the word James used, balance," I say.

"You asked James about this?" she says, looking back at me in the mirror.

"Yeah, he kind of said the same things as you," I say.

"Well, that's because Katie has used that word a lot when she explains her philosophy for her gym. She named it Perfect Balance for a reason."

"That's what James said, too!" I exclaim. "You guys are all in on this?" I accuse.

My mom laughs, "We are not in on anything. We are just all involved at PBGA because we agree with Katie. Alexis, I researched many gyms before you enrolled at PBGA."

"You did? I just thought we go there because it's the closest gym," I say.

"Well, that is a huge bonus, but no, I like the

way Katie runs her gym. And I am sure the parents and kids at Salt Lake Gymnastics like the way they run their gym. There is no right or wrong answer. PBGA was just the right answer for our family. "

"How do you know what is right for me? Maybe I should be at Salt Lake Gymnastics, competing this spring," I say, feeling ganged up on.

My mom is quiet for a minute and then she says, "I guess I don't Baby Girl, but let's stick with PBGA for a while longer and if you want to change gyms when you are older you can. But for now there's no rush."

I think about this silently as I look out the window. It's taking us longer to get home than usual because of the snow. It's coming down in large snowflakes. The roads are covered in snow except for tracks where the cars have made a groove. My mom is carefully driving in the tracks avoiding the snow so we don't slip. She is also driving extremely slow. I see snow plows up ahead coming down the hill on the other side of the road. The snow plows will be busy all night tonight.

I think again about what my mom and James said about balance and there being no rush. Why do adults always say that? There's no rush. They say that to kids, but adults seem to rush around more than anyone. And if there's no rush, then why are other teams training more than us?

"Alright," my mom says as she slowly turns into our drive. "I have a plate of food from dinner saved for you both in the fridge. You guys can heat it up while I finish helping Ethan with his science project."

We walk in and the house is quiet, for our house anyway. I'm not sure where Josh, Will, and Dad are, but I assume Ethan is working on his science project in his room because he has been growing something on his window sill.

I walk over to the kitchen sink to wash the chalk off my hands. Drew gets the save-plates out of the fridge and puts one in the microwave.

Then he comes over and starts washing his hands as I scoot over to dry my hands.

"Why would you want to go to Salt Lake Gymnastics anyway? They don't have a boys team," Drew points out.

"I thought you were listening to music," I say.

He gives me a grin, "I don't always turn it on," he admits.

"What?"

"You heard me," he says with a twinkle in his eye, "people say all sorts of crazy things when they think you aren't listening."

"How many people know about your little game?"

"Just you," he says as the microwave beeps. "Let's keep it that way, okay?" He goes over and takes out one plate of food and puts in another.

"Okay," I say. I look at my big brother who loves gymnastics too. I know I wouldn't really want to go to a gym that didn't have boys' gymnastics. I like having him in the gym with me during workout. And I'm glad I don't have to eat dinner alone when I get home from practice.

Chapter 4

Split Jump, Straight Jump on Beam

I smell the clean smell of ice and I feel the wind in my hair. My skis cut through the powder and there is snow up to my knees. I see the edge of the cliff in front of me and I don't turn my skis to stop myself. I keep heading straight for the cliff, and I'm not afraid to ski right off the edge. In fact, I feel peaceful and free. I pick up speed as I approach the edge of the cliff. Then I ski right off the edge and start flying. Suddenly my skis are not on my feet anymore. I am hanging on to them under my arms like they are a floatation device in water. I am flying, swaying back and forth in the breeze. I look down and see the mountains below me covered in snow, I can see chair lifts, the ski runs, the trees. It's so beautiful from up here. Everything is white -

Beep, beep, beep! I wake with a start and slap my alarm off.

I lay there for a moment wondering about the dream. We have been skiing a lot. Every Saturday since competition season ended. I skipped last Saturday because I had a little cold and wanted to rest. My dad was bummed about it, but I promised him the next three Saturdays and he recovered.

I slowly get up, thinking about how this is going to be a fun weekend with the banquet, the sleepover, and all this new snow for skiing. I get dressed in my green polo and khakis, the uniform at Mountain View Charter School. I am sitting on the floor of my room tying my shoes when my mom pops her head in, "Just making sure you're up," she says.

"I had the coolest skiing dream," I say as she leans into my room. "I can't wait to go this weekend since I missed last weekend."

"I assumed you wouldn't go this weekend either," she says.

"Why not?"

"Because of the sleepover."

"But that's Friday," I remind her.

She smiles a knowing smile and then says, "We'll see," and walks out to herd more kids down to breakfast.

I reach for my sweater to pull over my polo. Why does she think I won't go? Is it because she thinks I don't like it? I *want* to go skiing. With five kids in the family, skiing is the time my dad gets a moment with each of us. He takes turns riding up the chair lift with each of us and asks all sorts of questions. I love that time; riding high up above the ski runs, looking down on the trees, and talking to my dad. Even when there is a triple or quad chair he makes sure to rotate who he sits next to. He always has extra hand warmers and candy in his pockets.

I leave my room and trot down the stairs. My dad is sitting at the table with a slice of raisin bread and is scrolling through his phone.

"Hey Dad," I say.

"Alexis," he greets me back. "I hear you're not skiing tomorrow," he says setting his phone down.

"I'm skiing," I say.

"Really? Mom says you have the sleepover tonight."

"So?"

"So, I think you'll be too tired to ski tomorrow after all that debauchery," he explains.

"I won't stay up too late," I say sitting up to breakfast.

My mom walks in and starts setting out bowls. My dad clicks off his phone and starts to stand up to leave for work.

"Oh, Mark, are you leaving?" My mom asks and he nods. "Can you pick up the boys at basketball on your way to the banquet? I can meet you there with Alexis and Andrew."

"Why do we have to go?" Ethan whines as he walks into the room and sits up to the bar next to me.

"Because it's important we go as a family," my mom swiftly says. She turns and continues talking to my dad, "basketball ends at 6 and her banquet is at 6, so pick them up a few minutes early. We'll eat there. You're only getting Ethan and William, Josh will already be warming up for his game at the high school."

"Got it. 'Bye hon," he says leaning in and giving her a kiss before he heads out.

"Can we at least bring our tablets if we have to go to the dumb banquet?" Ethan continues.

My mom ignores him and yells, "Time for breakfast! Everyone down stairs!"

"Why are we doing Table Time on Friday?"
Will asks.

"Because we have a packed weekend," my
answers from the kitchen. "This is the only time we
have. Plus, you can get it over with and enjoy
your weekend."

We can hear her cutting up vegetables as
she adds, "You two need to hustle up too, Sarah
will be here any minute to pick you up."

It's Friday afternoon and instead of relaxing,
we are doing homework. My brothers, Ethan and
William, are in their basketball clothes ready to
be picked up for practice.

At that moment there's a honk outside and
the boys jump up and scramble out of the dining
room, "Bye Mom!" they yell over their shoulder,
as they run out the door.

My mom goes back to cutting up vegetables
for a salad she has to bring to the banquet. I

finish making my times table flash cards and walk into the kitchen. I climb up to the bar stool and watch her cut tomatoes for a moment.

"What's up Baby Girl?" she asks.

"Is Josh coming tonight?" I ask.

"No, he has a game," she answers. I figured he wasn't coming when I heard my mom and dad talking this morning. I rarely see Josh anymore.

"What should I wear?" I ask.

"I think it's going to be pretty casual. Just a potluck at the high school." She looks up at me, "Do you want to dress up?" she asks.

"Well, my gym friends only see me in a leotard, so I want to wear something nice," I confess.

My mom smiles, "I don't blame you. Nice is hard in this weather. I think you can be causal and cute. What about jeans and a sweater?" she says, sliding the tomato wedges into the salad with her knife.

"What about church clothes?" I ask, thinking

of some of my cute winter dresses.

"I think church clothes will be too fancy. I promise you will look nice in any of your sweaters."

"Okay," I say. I sit in silence for a minute watching her slice up a cucumber, until she looks up.

"What else Baby Girl?" she says.

"Dad says I'll be too tired to ski tomorrow," I confess.

"You will be too tired, and it's not safe to ski when you're tired. If you want to ski tomorrow, you need to come home from the sleepover early and go to bed here. Get some real rest. I could pick you up at 10 or 11 . . ."

"But I'm excited about the sleepover, I want to go to all of it," I say.

"Well, I think you can miss skiing this once. You have a fun night ahead of you. There will be other ski days."

"Yeah, but Dad has seemed so sad this year because we keep missing. Josh has only gone up like twice because of basketball," I point out.

"That's sweet of you to be worried about your dad, but he'll survive. There's enough of you to go around," she says. "Stop worrying and go upstairs and get changed. Pack for tonight too."

"Yeah, okay. Should I pack a leo?" I ask as I am getting down from the bar stool.

"Probably, or at least a tank and shorts. And some sweats to sleep in because that gym gets cold. And a toothbrush."

I nod and she is still rattling off things I need to pack as I head up the stairs. Leo, toothbrush, sweats, pillow. This sleepover is going to be awesome!

Chapter 5

Compulsories Team Banquet

My mom, Drew, and I arrive at Snowcap
Canyon High School for the team banquet and
I'm a little nervous. Drew and I follow my mom
through the corridors of the high school and

head for the cafeteria. Her heels are clicking along at a fast pace and we trail behind her because we're not walking as fast . . . no one walks as fast as she does.

We enter the cafeteria and we follow my mom over to a long table on the back wall where she sets down the salad with the rest of the food that everyone else brought.

"There's Trista! Can I go talk to her?" I ask.

"You can go talk to your friends Ba – Alexis, but you'll need to sit with your family when dinner and awards start, okay?"

"Okay," I agree.

"Andrew and I will find a table," she says, and they head off to find a table big enough for our family.

I walk over and greet Trista. She's with her parents and sister. We start talking about the talent show and what we want to create. "I don't know dance very well, but I brought some fun music that might work," Trista says.

"Hello everyone," Katie greets us from the

front of the room. The talking quiets down and she continues. "Thank you for coming to our Compulsory Team Banquet, which are Levels 3, 4, and 5. Our compulsory girls have worked hard this year and I look forward to recognizing each of them. But first let's start out by getting dinner. When everyone is seated with food, I'll start with awards," she says.

That's when I notice that there is a table behind her with trophies. *Ooh, I wonder who those are for. Is there one for me?*

"There are only six of 'em up there," Trista says reading my thoughts. "And way more than six of us here, so not everyone gets one."

I survey the room. The Level 3, 4, and 5 girls' teams are here tonight, so yes, way more than six gymnasts, more like 20.

"Guess this isn't basketball or baseball. No participation trophies for us," I say to Trista with a smile, although I am secretly bummed. My brothers get a trophy after every baseball and basketball season.

She smiles back, "It's way better. We are competitive, we don't want trophies just for showing up," she says. I smile back, but I'm not so sure.

"Let's eat so we can get to PNO sooner," I say and she nods and we part ways to eat with our families. I find my mom and Drew at our table. My Dad has arrived with William and Ethan.

"I peeked in on Josh warming up," I hear my dad telling my mom. Josh's game tonight is a home game here at the high school. "His game will probably start before this is done," he says looking at his watch.

"The game starts at seven. This could wrap up by then," my mom replies. "We can help move things along by filling our plates."

We follow her lead and fill our plates with all sorts of yummy food on the pot luck table. I put bread, pasta, and cookies on my plate. When we sit down my mom plops carrots on my plate, "Looks like you forgot these," she says.

I have a good time with my parents and my three brothers during dinner. Ethan and William are teasing Drew, as always, "No wonder you like gymnastics so much, dude, look at all these girls," William says elbowing Drew.

"Cut it out! That's not why I like gymnastics."

"It should be," Ethan says, "Maybe we should take up gymnastics," he teases.

"You wouldn't last," Drew says, "it's way harder than basketball or baseball."

"Yeah, right," William says, shoveling a huge bite of lasagna in his mouth.

"I challenge you to a handstand contest," Drew says

"I challenge you to a free throw contest," William retorts.

"Boys!" my mom says. "All sports at a high level are hard. None of you are at a high level yet so stop bickering." Then she looks at me and Drew sitting across from her and winks. We know our mom knows that gymnastics is way harder than any other sport.

Katie walks to the front of the room again and stands in front of the table of trophies. "Again, welcome everyone to our Compulsory Team Banquet. We have Levels 3, 4, and 5 here tonight. All three teams had a great season. We will start with awards for the Level 3 team and work our way up. Since James is the Level 3 coach, I will turn the time over to him." The parents clap as Katie sits down and James stands up.

He looks like he does at meets. He's not wearing his usual athletic pants with the stripes down the side and a t-shirt. Instead he's wearing nice jeans, a collared shirt, a sweater over the shirt, and dress shoes.

"Thanks, Katie," James says as he pulls a piece of paper out of his pocket. "I only had five girls on my Level 3 competition team this year. They are a fierce group. This group of girls took third place at the Utah State Meet this season. They were up against teams who had been competing Level 3 for two or three seasons. All of my Level 3s were rookies to competition. I'm very proud of all five of them and I would like them to come up here with me for a moment so I can talk about each of them."

I look to my mom questioningly. "Go on up Baby – Alexis" she whispers. I do as she says and stand up and make my way to the front of the room, I see that my teammates are doing the same. As we are walking toward James the parents start clapping for us. This is a little embarrassing and I can feel my cheeks turn pink as I walk up to James.

"Hi ladies," he says to us as we stop in front of him. "Why don't you line up shoulder to shoulder and face the parents while I talk about you," he says. He quickly arranges us facing the parents.

"So here are my little Level 3s," he says and the audience chuckles.

"I'm going to talk a minute about each of them. Let's start with Red, I mean Paige," he says and the parents laugh. He walks over and picks up a certificate that has gold trim and I see it says Perfect Balance Gymnastics Academy at the top with the logo of the gymnast leaping over the snowflake in the middle. There is smaller print across the middle that I can't read.

"I give Paige the Team Captain Award. She kept this team calm during a stressful State Meet. She helped my little ones know what to do and where to go during competition and she keeps these girls on task during practice. Paige is a born leader and we are lucky to have her on the team." He shakes Paige's hand and gives her the certificate. Paige quietly takes it and the parents clap.

"Next we have Marissa," he says, since Marissa is standing next to Paige. "Marissa is a no-nonsense athlete. Actually, Marissa is a no-nonsense person." At this the parents laugh. "Marissa quietly works hard every day and she is Miss Consistent in meets. This girl competes her routines exactly how she trains them in practice. This is a rare quality in such a young competitor. So, Marissa, I debated giving you Miss Consistent or the Nerves of Steel Award," he says, walking over to pick up the certificate. "And then I decided the combination of both makes you MVP, Most Valuable Player." With this he picks up one of the trophies and hands it to her. She beams as she takes the trophy and the parents clap.

"Okay, Alexis," he says walking to stand behind me. I stand there quietly looking at my parents, I'm worried about what he's going to say. "Lexi had a great season, but what I enjoy most about Lex is her attitude. She is happy every day she comes into the gym. She gets along with all her teammates and she works hard. Lex also had her first big crash, and although she really didn't want to, she got back up on that beam and tried again."

He walked over to the table and picked up a certificate. "Lexi, I give you the Best Attitude Award." The parents clap as I take the certificate from him. My mom jumps up out of her chair and is standing and clapping. I know that getting Best

Attitude has made her just as happy, maybe even happier, than getting an MVP award.

"Who's next?" He says looking at our line. "Savannah? Savannah –Anna?" He says walking behind Savannah and putting his hand on her shoulder. "This little sprite is fun to watch compete. She barely clears the beam with the top of her head." The parents chuckle as he says this. "And it would be easy for me to give her the Cutie Pie Award. But Anna is more than just a Cutie Pie. She works hard, and tries her skills in different ways when I ask her to. I also experiment with new drills on Savannah and she is a good sport about it. I give Savannah the Most Coachable Award."

He hands her the certificate and Savannah's mom yells, "That's my Cutie Pie!" and everyone laughs.

"Last, but not least, Trista. This girl is trouble," he says and we all laugh. I can see Trista bouncing on her toes slightly and I can tell she can barely stand it. "Triss is my fire cracker. I never know what I'm going to get when this girl walks in for practice. But I will say this, Trista has learned to work hard this year. She started off goofing around and only wanting to work what she's good at. Now she works the hardest on her weakest event and she has improved tremendously on all events. So Trista, you have earned the Most Improved Award," he says picking up a trophy and handing it to her.

"Ladies and Gentleman," James announces as he walks behind us, "I present to you your new Perfect Balance Gymnastics Academy Level 4s!" I look at my teammates and they seem as stunned and happy as I am. We are all moving up together!

The parents clap loudly for all of us and James excuses us to go back to our seats. As I get back to my seat my mom grabs my hand and squeezes it. I know she is proud of me without her saying anything. My dad leans over to me and whispers "Gotta go Alexis, great job, catch you at home," I nod to him and he sneaks out with Ethan and William. I know they are going to Josh's basketball game, which has started by now. I see Drew does not get up with them and I look at him and raise my eyebrows at him; he winks back. So Drew is staying for me. He's the best. I smile and turn my attention back to James.

"Can I get my *old* Level 4 girls up here?" he says. James coaches Level 4 and 5 with Melony. When he is coaching us, Melony has them. James begins talking about the Level 4s in the same way he talked about us and the parents are enjoying themselves. Just like our team, he gives out two trophies. One MVP and one Most Improved.

But I can't really focus on what he is saying because I want so badly for this to be over so we can get to our sleepover. The sleepover is with all three teams, but I mostly want to play with my teammates and make up a routine for the talent show.

Finally, James is done talking about the Level

4s and he sits down and lets Melony talk about the Level 5 team. When Melony is done giving out the awards for Level 5 Katie stands up again.

"Before we wrap this up and let the girls start their sleepover I think there is one more group we need to recognize. Ladies, I want you to turn to the person who drives you to practice two or three times a week. I want you to thank them." There is some giggling and thank yous murmured. I look at my mom and whisper 'thanks' and she smiles. "Without your driver, your cook, your-leotard-buying parents, there would be no gymnastics. So, from the bottom of my heart, I would like to thank all of you for supporting your child in this wonderful sport and I look forward to another great season next year." The parents clap briefly and people start getting up to leave.

Chapter 6

Cartwheel on Beam

Paige bounces up to me as we are leaving the banquet, "Hey Lexi, I've been working on a routine and I have so many ideas for your show."

"Really?" I say, "That's great!"

"Yeah, did you pack music? Are you headed straight over?" She asks.

"Yes – "

"Actually," my mom cuts in, "I was planning

on watching the rest of Josh's game before I take you over."

"How long will that take?" I ask. I don't want to wait until Josh's game is over. This is the problem with having so many brothers.

She looks at her watch, "Maybe another hour or so."

"An hour!" I exclaim.

"Alexis, your team will be there all night, an hour is not going to be a big deal."

"It is to me," I fuss.

"Why don't you catch a ride with Paige or someone?" my brother pipes in.

I look at Drew. He is brilliant.

I turn to Paige, "Can I ride with you?" I blurt out as if my life depended on it.

"Probably, we're headed straight there. I'll go ask," she says and turns to go find her mom.

"I didn't know you were so anxious Baby Girl, or I would've helped you arrange a ride earlier," my mom says.

"Can I go with her for the PNO part?" Drew

asks.

"You don't want to watch Josh's game?" my mom asks.

Drew shrugs, "I'd rather be at the gym," he confesses.

"Alright, you two gym rats, you can both go now. Andrew, why don't you run out and get Alexis' overnight bag from the car," she says handing him the keys. "Alexis and I will find out who can give you a ride."

In the end, we caught a ride with Savannah's mom, Debi. But Debi made us pose for pictures before we could leave. By the time we were done taking pictures my mom had left to watch Josh's game and Drew was back with my overnight bag and his gym bag. He plopped them at his feet and waited for us to finish.

"Mom, can we go now?" Savannah pleads.

"Yes, I just wanted a few good pictures of you girls all dressed up," she says.

"Where's your brother? We're taking him too, right?" she asks.

"He's over by the door," I say.

Debi chuckles, "Okay, let's go."

We pile in the car and the entire ride over Savannah's mom is chattering about the other levels and who got MVP and Most Improved from the other teams. I'm surprised she knows so much about the other teams and who is good at what. My mom knows gymnastics, but she doesn't really know the girls on the Level 4 and 5 teams.

When we get to Perfect Balance Savannah's mom parks and walks us in. Drew and I thank her for the ride and head toward the cubbies. I can hear Savannah's mom saying, "Honey, I want you to have fun, but I also want you to work cartwheels on beam tonight, okay?"

"Okay," Savannah agrees.

"See you in the morning, have fun. Call me if you want me to come get you," her mom adds.

"Okay. 'Bye Mom!" Savannah says giving her mom a hug and then she joins us by the cubbies.

"Why does your mom want you to work cartwheels?" I ask, as I stuff my overnight bag into a cubbie.

"Because I want to do Level 4 this fall," Savannah answers.

"But you heard James, we all just officially moved up to Level 4."

"Yeah, but we need to have all of our Level 4 skills if we want to compete," she explains.

"Maybe I'll do some with you," I say.

"What about your talent show routine?" she asks. I look through the glass doors into the gym. PNO is in full swing; it's a zoo. There are kids everywhere.

"Maybe we work on it when the gym clears out and it's just us for the sleepover?" I suggest.

"Hey guys," Paige says walking up, "have you figured out where you're sleeping tonight?"

"The pit!" Savannah says with enthusiasm.

"The pit? That might not be as comfortable as it looks," Paige points out.

"Maybe we can put four 8-inchers together and sleep in a circle?" I suggest.

"That would be good," Paige says setting her

stuff down and rummaging through her bag. She pulls out her phone and starts scrolling through it. "I brought a bunch of songs for us to pick from for our dance," she says.

"You did?"

"Yeah, sure. Let's go listen to my dance playlist." We walk into the training area and head over to floor where the sound system is. When we get to the stereo we pull out the gym phone and plug in her phone.

"Hey!" Aaron yells at us from the boys' events. "We were listening to that!"

"We are always listening to your music, Aaron," Paige fires back. "I promise we'll play good workout tunes," she assures him. He looks at her for a moment and then gives a brief nod and goes back to swinging on the P-bars.

"Here, you scroll through Alexis, it's your talent show," Paige says handing me her phone.

I scroll through her music, she has a lot of different choices and I don't recognize most of them. Then I see one I know. "How about <u>Roar</u> by

Katy Perry?" I suggest.

"Play it. Let's see," she says.

I click on the song. As it comes on I remember that I really like this song. It seems perfect. The words are about being strong and your own hero. I look at Paige and she is bopping up and down to the music.

"It's too slow," she decides. "Great song though. What else?" she looks at me.

I look back down at her playlist and let "Roar" keep playing while I continue scrolling. I'm looking for something familiar when Trista walks up.

"This is a great song! Is this what we're doing our dance to?" she asks.

"Paige says it's too slow," Savannah supplies.

"I wouldn't know. You can just put me in for the tumbling parts," she says.

Trista and Paige used to get so mad at each other over dance class, but somewhere along the way they decided to get along and I like it so much better. As I'm scrolling I see "All About the

Bass" by Meghan Trainor. "How about this one?" I ask.

"Let's hear," Paige says.

I tap on the song and half the kids in the gym yell at us for turning off Katy Perry and the other half are happy about the new song. Paige listens for a minute.

"I think it's too slow too, plus I think the words are too grown up. We don't want to go through the trouble of making up an entire routine and then have parents tell us the song doesn't work."

"Really? The words are bad?" I ask. I hadn't ever listened to the words.

"Not bad, just older. Keep looking. It's slow anyway," Paige says.

"Okay," I say scrolling down some more, "what about 'Timber' by Pitbull and Ke$ha?" I ask.

"Oh, that one's good! Try it," Paige says.

I touch the screen and the song starts coming out of the speakers. Again, some kids yell at us and some kids like the new song. Paige starts tapping her foot and swaying to the song.

"This one is really good," she says.

"I still like the idea of Katy Perry," Savannah adds, "everyone likes Katy Perry."

Paige is moving now, and I am jealous at how she can feel the music so easily. I look at her questioningly. She seems to really like this one. I need Paige to love it. She is the only one good enough to make up a great routine.

"Sure, we can keep looking. There's more Katy on there," she says.

I keep scrolling and I find another Katy Perry song, "Part of Me." I don't ask this time, I just hit the screen and Katy Perry replaces Pitbull and Ke$ha. By now the kids in the gym have given up on us changing the music so much.

"This is a break-up song though," Trista says. "My sister listened to it over and over when a dumb boy broke up with her."

"But does it have to be?" Marissa asks. This is the first I've heard from Marissa. I didn't even see her walk up.

"What do you mean?" I ask her.

"Well, it kind of reminds me of, like, other kids making fun of us for doing gymnastics. Like Savannah's mean girls at Hilltop. And we will be performing gymnastics, and saying, this is part of us. Listen to the words," she says.

We quiet down and concentrate on the words.

"Like no matter what other kids say, they can't take gymnastics away from us?" Savannah clarifies.

"Exactly," Marissa says.

"It's perfect."

Chapter 7

Standing Back Tuck into the Pit

"Will the beat work, Paige?" I ask. My teammates and I are trying to figure out what music to use in my school's talent show.

"It's not as good as 'Timber,' but it'll work. Do you guys want this one?"

We all nod yes, not sure how this is going to work.

"Put the song on repeat and let's go over to the mirrors," Paige instructs.

I tap on the repeat icon, set the phone down, and we all walk over to the mirrors. We start dancing around and messing with ideas. Trista and Savannah lose interest after the song loops a couple of times.

"Hey, do you guys care if we go play on the tramp for a bit? You can get us when you have something to teach us."

"Sure," Paige says. "Do you guys want to go play too?" She asks Marissa and me.

"No, this is fun," Marissa says.

"No, it's my talent show, I want to help," I say.

"Okay. Well, this is what I've got so far," Paige says. "First, we each start here, but begin dancing at different times. I start at the one, Marissa at five, Trista at one, Savannah at five and you come in last at the one. Then we all do the chorus together, dancing over here to each do a tumbling pass or leap pass."

"Okay, can you teach it to us so we can try

it?" I ask.

"Yeah, let me show you and Marissa first and if it looks good we can teach it to those two," she says, referring to Trista and Savannah.

"There are 64-counts before we get to the chorus. We'll do a roll off starting 4-counts apart and doing an 8-count sequence, taking up 32 counts. Then we do another 16-count sequence twice together and then we tumble during the chorus. I'll teach you the roll off part," she says.

Paige teaches Marissa and I the beginning roll off part and the three of us try it over and over until we have it down. By this time other kids are starting to complain that they are sick of listening to the same song over and over.

"Girls," the teenage coach that is working PNO walks over to us, "we have to change the music until PNO is over. You are driving us all nuts."

Marissa runs over and unplugs Paige's phone and plugs in the gym phone. The soundtrack from *Moana* start blaring through the speakers.

I sit down, sad that we have to stop working on the routine for now.

"We have all night Lex. We can work on it some more when this place clears out. In the meantime, let's teach Trista and Savannah the beginning," Paige suggests.

We round up Trista and Savannah and teach them the 20 counts of the roll off.

"When do we tumble?" Trista asks.

"During the chorus. We can make sure you and Lexi tumble the most," Paige says. This makes Trista smile and she goes back to trying to learn the dance again. I can tell learning the dance moves are hard and not fun for her. I'm so glad she is doing it anyway.

We don't work on the dance for very long because we can't try it with the music. We decide to go play on the equipment. We run into some of the Level 4 and 5 girls waiting for a turn on the trampoline. Most of them are staying for the team sleepover too. After we all get a turn on trampoline Savannah asks me if I will work

PERFECT BALANCE GYMNASTICS SERIES

cartwheels with her. I agree and we walk over to the beam area.

"Savannah, don't you get most of your skills pretty easily?" I ask her.

"I guess, but my mom is worried about it because I have a hard time on beam during meets."

"Oh," I say. If Savannah is worried about a cartwheel, maybe I should be worried too.

We get to the low beams, I step up onto one and Savannah steps up onto another. We start doing cartwheels. We invent a game to see how many times we can get both feet on at the end of the skill without stepping off.

"Working beam cartwheels, that's what I like to see," James says walking into the gym. He's no longer in his fancy dad clothes, but back in sweat pants and his Under Armor sweatshirt.

"Are you staying over James?" Savannah asks.

"Naw, I'm just going to play for a little while and go home and sleep in my comfy bed while you guys torture Melony and Katie all night. Lexi, make sure you look under your second arm on those cartwheels, okay?" I nod and he smiles and keeps walking into the gym. I'm sure he is headed to give other kids corrections even though he's not technically working PNO.

Then my mom steps into the gym, "Hey Alexis, can you go get your brother for me?" she asks. I look around the gym and see him over by the pit with Trista. I trot across the floor over to them.

"Drew, Mom's here," I say.

"Okay. Let's do one more," he says and Trista nods. They both stand on the edge of the floor with their back to the pit. Then he counts out 1,2,3 and they both do a standing back tuck into the pit. They think this is hilarious as they climb out of the pit. I am envious that they can both do a standing back tuck, even if it is just into the pit.

"Come on, Drew, you know Mom will get mad if you don't go when she gets here."

"Yeah," he agrees. "Have fun tonight you two," he says and runs across the floor and through the doors into the lobby to get his stuff. I walk back over to my mom.

"Do you have everything you need Ba-Alexis?" she asks.

I grin, she is trying so hard not to say Baby Girl in public. "Yeah. And we already made up a bunch of the routine for the talent show," I say.

"You're trying out?" she asks. I can tell she is happy about my decision to participate in the talent show. She has been trying to get me into shows and plays for years and I could never make it past tryouts. This time will be different and she will be so proud.

"Yeah, we're trying out," I answer.

"Alexis, you have to tell me so we can sign you up for try outs on Wednesday," she says.

"There are sign ups?" I ask.

"Yes, but if you're sure you want to do it, I'll help you fill out the form this weekend."

"I do, and my teammates are doing it with me," I say.

"Did you ask their parents?"

"No," I confess.

"Okay, I'll call everyone tonight to see if they can all be at your school on Wednesday for tryouts and for the night of the show. I'll text you if someone can't be in it so you guys can change it, okay?"

"Thanks Mom," I say, I didn't think about how my friends would get to tryouts and stuff like that.

"Sure, now give me a hug," she grins.

I walk over and lean into her. "I'm proud of you for trying for the show. Be a good girl for Melony and please go to bed before midnight, okay?" she pleads.

"Maybe," I say with a grin.

Drew is waiting for us silently. She turns to him, "Ready handsome?" she asks. He rolls his eyes and nods.

They walk out and within a few minutes the last of the kids for PNO get picked up. The gym becomes eerily quiet and feels so big. The Level 4 and 5 girls are dragging mats out to the middle of the floor and seem to be setting up an obstacle course. At least they left some space in front of the mirror.

Chapter 8

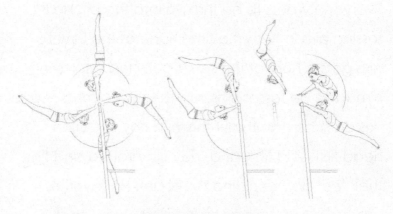

Tkatchev on Bars
(also called a Reverse Hecht)

"It's kind of spooky this quiet, huh?" Marissa points out. Parents' Night Out has just ended and we are staying for our team sleepover. We have never seen the gym this empty.

All of a sudden we feel water hit our backs.
We squeal and look around and there is James
holding a giant water gun, "Let's get this party
started!" he yells and soaks us again with water.
Girls are running and screaming and going every
which way. Some girls run at him to try to get the
water gun. He easily picks them up and tosses
them in the pit. Then this becomes the game.
Everyone wants to be thrown into the pit. He is
tossing girls in two at a time. One of the Level 5
girls gets a hold of the squirt gun and is spraying
him while he tosses girls into the pit. Gymnasts are
like cats, he can throw them in any direction,
head first, side first, and they flip around and find
their feet before hitting the foam. His favorite, it
seems, is grabbing an ankle and a wrist and
winging the girls in sideways.

I am standing still watching this mayhem
when Katie walks up, "James! They are not
allowed to get hurt! And you are getting my
equipment wet!"

He turns and grabs her and, without

hesitating, tosses her in! This makes all the girls squeal with delight. We have never seen anyone treat Katie as anything other than the boss lady around here.

"James! You tyrant! You are going to pay!" She says climbing out of the pit.

"I'd like to see you try," he challenges.

"That's it girls, it's us against him! He's going down!" At this declaration, his eyes widen and he has the good sense to run. He doesn't get far before a pack of girls tackle him and start dragging him toward the pit. This is no easy task, even for all these strong little girls. Plus, he starts tickling them and they become worthless in their attempt to push him to the pit, but they do drag him down to his knees and then girls start jumping on his back and he collapses dramatically to his stomach. He rolls over to his back as Katie walks up and sets one foot on his chest. "Do you surrender to PBGA Women?" she asks with her hands on her hips.

"Never!" and he reaches up and grabs her

ankle and picks up her foot to make her fall off balance, but she is so flexible she just stands there, with her ankle in his hand. He sits up and lifts her leg up above his head and she just grins, "PBGA Women rule! Admit it!" She remains in balance with her hands on her hips.

"You realize I am outnumbered here. If I had the boys team with me, it would be a different story."

"I repeat, do you surrender to PBGA Women?"

He pauses, looks at the girls around him and drops her leg, lifts his arms, palms out in a surrender sign and smiles. "I surrender," he says, laughing, "no one stands a chance with you ladies."

At this the girls cheer and begin to climb off him to go play on the trampoline.

"You going to spot me on 'katchevs?" Katie asks James.

"Did you bring grips?" he asks.

"Of course," she answers.

"Well, grip up, let's do this," he says standing up.

"What are 'katchevs?'" Marissa asks.

"It's short for Tkatchev or reverse hecht. It's a Level 9/10 release move on bars," he explains.

"You're going to do gymnastics for us?" I ask Katie.

"Not for you, with you. And, of course, I'll do gymnastics, that's why I own a gym," she says.

Marissa and I grin at each other, this is going to be fun. We walk over to our teammates who are waiting in line for the trampoline to tell them that Katie is going to do release moves on bars. By the time we make our way back over to the pit Katie is climbing up onto the pit bar. She swings back and forth a few times to get a feel for the bar and then she does a kip, cast handstand, giant, giant, fly away.

Holy cow, I had no idea Katie could do all that!

"Ugh, I'm too old for the pit," she says as she is climbing out of the pit. "Will you girls go get an

8-incher for me to throw in?" she asks.

I nod and hustle off with my teammates to grab an 8-incher from the middle of the floor. We quickly drag it across the floor so we don't miss seeing any of Katie's skills.

Chapter 9

Giant Swing on Bars

We are at our team sleepover and James is standing on the floor in coach mode. Only this time he is not coaching us, he is coaching the owner, Katie. We have brought him a mat she requested and he takes it from us and tosses it into the pit where Katie will be landing. "Do you need one more warm-up or do you want to go for it before your hands burn out?" he asks, as he straightens out the mat from the edge of the floor.

"Can you stand there for a timer?" she asks, climbing up to the bar that is over the pit.

"Sure," he says and he starts climbing up the ladder to the spotting platform. Katie steps off the platform and swings a few times. Then she does a kip up to a support position. She makes the kip look so easy. Just a way to get up onto the bar. Which it is, but it's so much harder than she makes it look.

She looks up at James standing on the spotting platform. "On the second giant I'll do a timer and fall into the pit. You can get the feel for the bump," she says referring to James' job as a spotter.

"I know how to spot these; you just get the

feel for yourself. Don't worry about me," he says.

She grins, "Okay," then she casts to handstand and does a giant. When she is at the top of the bar I see James grab her arm as she swings into the second giant. As she reaches the top of the bar where the second giant would normally end in a handstand, she arches her back and he puts the palm of his other hand on her back. Her shoulders are over the bar, but the rest of her body is parallel with the floor. She stops in this position for just a second and then twists and falls to her feet on the mat in the pit.

"Stronger tap so I don't have to do all the work," James says. Katie nods as she steps off the mat and heads over to the chalk trays.

"I'm ready if you are," she says. He nods. "I'm not going to try to catch the bar, I just want to sail over and get the feel of it," she says.

"Okay," he nods. Then he looks around and yells, "No jumping in the pit for the next few minutes, okay everyone?" he yells.

We agree, although, I don't know why he has

bothered. Most of us have stopped playing to watch what she is going to do. She jumps up to the bar does a couple of swings into a kip, cast handstand, giant. On the second giant she does the same arch at the top of the bar but instead of stopping she lets go of the bar. James has his hand on her back as she flies over the bar, lifts her chest, straddles, and reaches her hands for the bar. But she is about a foot away from catching and she lands feet first into the pit.

"Holy cow, that was totally awesome!" Trista yells.

"That was *sick!*" one of the Level 5 girls says.

Katie smiles, "Thanks girls. I'm going to try a few more."

"Did you ever compete that?" a girl asks.

"Yep, my senior year in high school and in college," she answers with pride.

"Okay, Chatty Kathy, let's go again," James yells down from the spotting platform.

Katie sticks her tongue out at James, but does as he says and climbs up to the spotting platform. She does the release move again, this time just a few inches from catching the bar. James gives her a correction so she can catch the bar on her next try.

"I'm only doing one more and then some tumbling." He nods in agreement as she gets onto a support position on the bar. This time she skips the kip and starts with a cast handstand. Then she does a giant, giant into a Tkachev. James bumps her up as she sails over the bar, she lifts her chest rotates a little forward and reaches for the bar. With a loud smack, her hands connect with the bar. We cheer and yell and she swings into a kip and stops in a support on the bar. She looks up at James and they high five each other.

"Let's end on that one," he says. She nods and casts to handstand, does a half pirouette and falls into the pit.

"Thanks James. Floor?" she asks looking up at him from her mat in the pit.

"Sure," he agrees. "Ladies, clear the

diagonal," he yells as he starts climbing down from the spotting platform.

I look at Marissa, who is standing next to me. "The cheese?" she says referring to the wedge-shaped mat closest to us that is sitting on the diagonal. I nod. Cheese mats are awkward to lift, so we push it to the edge of the floor so it's no longer sitting on the diagonal.

Katie starts undoing her grips as she walks across the floor to the coaches' offices. She opens the office door, throws her grips on a desk and comes back to the floor. By the time she gets back most of the mats are out of the way. She starts warming up her tumbling and some of the girls join her, including Trista, but I'm having fun just watching. I can't wait to tell Drew what a great gymnast Katie is, I'm not sure any of us knew. Although, she does have her college posters up in the parent viewing area. I wonder if my mom was as good as Katie?

Once Katie is warmed up she walks over to the side of the floor so she can tumble into the pit. James spots her on double backs into the pit. Then she does some double layouts and, my favorite, some Arabian double fronts.

"What is that called again?" Trista asks.

"Arabian double front," Katie answers

"I'm going to compete that someday," Trista promises.

"It's hard to land. It's a skill that takes a lot of practice Trista, you up for it?"

"Yes, I'll do whatever it takes and whatever you tell me," Trista says sincerely.

"I'm going to remember those words, Triss," Katie teases. "Okay, girls, I'm spent for now. That was enough gymnastics to keep me happy and make me sore tomorrow."

"What about beam?" I ask. "Can you still do beam?"

Katie smiles, "Yeah, I can still do beam, but I'm tired now. Maybe later tonight."

We all whine and moan and try to cajole her into showing us some beam stuff, but she plops down.

"You guys, I'm 28, which is old for a gymnast. I don't train the skill everyday like you do, cut me some slack." We understand that nothing we can say at this point will change her mind so girls start leaving her side to start playing on the equipment again.

"Did you compete with my mom?" I ask her.

"No, she's a little older than me and I went to a different college than her. But I remember watching her compete for BYU when I was a kid," she says.

"You do? Was she as good as you?"

"Better," Katie says, "ask to see old videos of her beam routine. She had the most beautiful switch, switch side."

I'm silent for a moment. How do I not know this about my mom? And what is a switch, switch side?

"I hear you're putting together a dance routine," she says changing the subject.

"It's for my school talent show."

"Cool, let's see it."

"Okay," I say looking around, my teammates are all close by trying to spot each other on back tucks into the pit. "Katie wants to see our dance routine," I say to them.

"But we aren't done," Marissa points out.

"I know, but she just wants to see what we have so far," I explain.

"You're going to love it," Trista says as they walk to their starting spots on the floor in front of the mirrors. Katie moves to sit on some panel mats in front of the mirrors so we are facing her. Marissa runs over to the stereo system and turns on the song.

Chapter 10

Back Extension Roll on Floor

We are standing in position, ready to show off our dance routine to Katie. The music starts and we try the roll off, but we all began at the wrong time.

"Stop, stop!" Paige yells. "You guys did the moves right but I don't think you're counting out the song. It begins, 5, 6, 7, 8 and Katy Perry starts singing at the one. That's when I start dancing and then we go down the line. If you are confused, just remember Katy starts singing on the one, okay?" We all nod. She looks at Marissa and Marissa runs over to start the song again.

This time Paige yells the numbers at us when the song starts, "5, 6, 7, 8 and 1, 2, 3, 4, 5, 6, 7, 8 and 1, 2, 3, 4, 5, 6, 7, 8 . . . "

We all seem to start at the right time and it looks so cool in the mirrors. When we are done with that 16-count section Trista jumps up and down, "Paige! That looked so cool, this is going to be great. Do you love it Lex?" she asks me.

"Yeah, I do," I say, with a grin.

"It looks cool you guys," Katie says standing up. "Great song. Come get me when you're all done. Awesome start."

"Thanks," Paige says and Katie leaves to go see what the Level 4 and 5 girls are doing.

"Can we learn the rest Paige?" I ask.

Paige is beaming at how well we are doing, "Of course. It's really simple. You just have to learn 32 counts and we'll repeat it." She says. "When we're all done with the roll off we are facing the front." We all face the front in our staggered formation she has put us in. Then she teaches us 16 new counts and it takes us a while to learn it.

"Marissa, why don't you put the song on repeat?" Paige suggest.

We try the 32 counts over and over while the song is on repeat. Then Paige explains how we take 4-counts to move in to position to do tumbling passes. She put Trista and Savannah on one end and me, Marissa, and herself on the other end.

"I think Trista and I should go at the same time," Paige instructs. "Trista can tumble toward the front of the stage and me at the back. We'll cross each other without hitting, and then it's Savannah and Marissa's turn to go. Lexi, you go by yourself since it's your school."

We all agree to this. Tumbling at the same time across from each other is no big deal, we do it all the time in practice. We know how to avoid hitting each other.

"What should we do in the tumbling part?" Trista asks.

"Let's start with cartwheel-cartwheels, then round offs, leaps, round off back handsprings. At the end we can do back handspring, back handsprings, and Trista can end with her back tuck."

We agree to this and practice doing it a few times. Then we decide to try the entire thing to the music. When we added in the tumbling we learned that doing up to the back handspring takes up the time span of the chorus. Paige decides to repeat the 64 counts from the beginning and then we tumble again during the second chorus. To make the tumbling fit the chorus we decide to do round off back handsprings, leaps, two back handsprings and hitch kick cartwheels.

After the second chorus Paige teaches me a little twirl to the front so I can dance to the part where the words say to look at me. Then I do a little 4-count in front by myself before I join the group again. We repeat our usual 64-count dance and then for the third chorus we decide to have free passes and do whatever we want so that it looks a little crazy. The song ends with a fourth chorus and we do our 64-count. We have to be faster to this part of the song and it is harder to do, but we eventually get it. At the very end I do my twirl to the front again and we all hit a pose when the song ends. Me in the middle with one arm up and one on my hip and two of my teammates on either side of me.

"Should we have two up, two down?" Marissa asks as we look at our ending formation in the mirror.

"Yeah, let's keep Lexi standing in the middle and Paige and I on either side of her on our knees. Savannah and Marissa you can stand on the outer edges," Trista suggests.

We try that and look in the mirror. We look good, all rosy cheeked and muscled.

"This is awesome!" I burst out. "Let's try the whole thing for Katie!"

We call Katie over, she is sitting on the edge of the tumble track while James is spotting some girls on double backs on the trampoline. She looks over to us and grins, then gets up and walks over to us.

"Are you guys ready to show everyone?" she asks.

"Everyone?" Paige says.

"Yeah, the gym, me, Melony, James, the Level 4s and 5s. Everyone," She repeats.

"Let's just show you first," Marissa smartly responds.

"Well, you guys have to do it in front of an entire school. Better practice on us first. Plan on doing it for everyone at some point tonight," she says.

This makes my stomach sink a little. *Can I do*

this in front of my entire school? Then I look at my friends lining up in front of the mirrors in their starting positions and I know I can do it with them on stage with me.

I move to stand in formation with them. The music starts and Paige counts it out for us the entire time. We do the roll off, the dance sequence, the tumbling, the dance, tumbling again, and end with the fast dancing, crazy tumbling, and the final pose.

"Yay!" Katie says clapping. "It's so cute, you guys are wonderful! I'm impressed you made it up in one night."

"That was all Paige," I say.

"You're very talented Paige," Katie says to her. "Have you ever taken dance classes?"

"Just the ones here," Paige answers.

"I'm not sure that counted until Julia got here. Impressive routine, especially with your limited training," she says. "I only have one correction for you guys."

"What?" I ask.

"Hold the ending pose for three seconds," she suggests.

"Okay," I agree.

"Do you guys want to try it in front of everyone?" Trista asks.

"Not really," I admit. The Level 4 and 5 girls are older and cooler kids. What if they think it's dumb?

"Why not?" Trista asks, "It's a totally awesome routine and we need to practice."

I grab the ends of my short hair and start twirling it around my fingers. Trista is looking at me, waiting for an answer. I give her a small nod and she gives me a giant grin back.

"Hey everyone!" she yells to the gym, "Come over here for a quick show!"

Girls stop what they're doing on the equipment, walk over to the mirrors, and sit down in front of us. My teammates go to their starting spots and Katie walks over the stereo system to start the song for us.

We do the routine all the way through with

the tumbling and everything. When we are holding the ending pose, like Katie told us to, the girls start clapping.

"That was really good," one of the girls says standing up.

"Who made that up?" another girl asks.

"Paige did it," Savannah says.

Paige is smiling and enjoying the praise from the older girls.

"Do you guys need to run through it a few more times?" Katie asks.

"It's up to you," Marissa says to me.

"How about a couple more times so we all remember it next week," I suggest.

We do the entire routine three times through until we are exhausted. We're sitting on the floor talking about how fun the talent show is going to be when suddenly the lights flicker.

Chapter 11

Compulsories Team Sleepover

"Girls!" Katie yells from the glass doors where the light switches are located. "It's 2am, time to get out sleeping bags and pillows and make your nest. I'm turning lights out in 30 minutes." We look at each other, we never decided how or where we are going to sleep.

"Let's just grab some 8-inchers and put them in a circle" Marissa suggests.

"I wanted to sleep in the pit," Savannah says.

"I promise, Anna, that's not going to be comfortable," Paige says to her.

"What about the resi-pit?" Trista suggests.

"Still too smooshy," Paige says.

"Come on you guys, let's get 8-inchers before they are all gone," Marissa says. We follow her eyes and we see all the Level 4 and 5 girls have already moved the 8-inch mats to the middle of the floor and are rolling their sleeping bags out onto them.

"There's one left under the far beam!" Trista yells and we start running over, but we are too late, some Level 5s get to it before us.

"Guess you guys will have to use panel mats," one of the girls says as they drag the last 8-incher out from under the beams.

We stand there stunned.

"We got distracted doing your dumb routine and now all the mats are taken," Trista blurts out.

"It's not dumb!" I yell back at her.

"What is the problem?" James says walking up. "Just grab 4-inchers. Geez, where are your problem solving skills?"

"4-inchers?" Marissa says. We look around again and see two 4-inchers under the high bar. They are full of chalk, but they are our last hope for a comfortable night. Without a word to each other we run over to the high bar, pull out the 4-inchers and drag them between the beams to the floor. We arrange the mats so that three of us are on one and two of us are on the other. Our heads are together.

"Now that you five have that figured out, I'm going to take off," James says. "Try not to give Katie any trouble and clean up in the morning so you can do this again next year."

"Okay," we say.

"Night ladies,"

"Night," we say back and he turns and heads

out.

"So, tell me all your secrets!" Trista says, propping up on her elbows.

"Who are you talking to?" Marissa asks.

"All of you. Isn't this the time to share all the dirt?" Trista grins.

"We're nine, we don't have dirt," I say.

"Good night everyone!" Katie yells and flicks the lights off. The gym becomes dark except for small slivers of moonlight from the windows.

"Well, who do you like?" Trista whispers in the dark.

"Like a boy?" I whisper back.

"Yeah, is there a boy at school you think is cute?"

"I guess. There's this boy, Sean, who is nice to me. Not at all like my brothers." I confess.

"Is he your boyfriend?" Savannah asks.

"I don't think so. How does that work?" I ask.

"He just asks you to be his girlfriend and you say yes," Paige supplies. "But most boys don't ask that question until 5th or 6th grade," she adds.

"Well, now what do I do about him?" I ask.

"You could ask him to be your boyfriend," Trista says.

"Have you done that?" I ask Trista. I will be impressed, but not surprised if Trista says yes.

But Trista looks down and says, "No, I'm too chicken he'll say no," and then she looks at Paige and they exchange a look.

"What?" I say.

"Nothing," Trista mumbles.

"Triss, you're scared of something?" Marissa says in mock horror and we all giggle.

"Girls!" Katie yells over to us, "Time to sleep."

With that we lay our heads down on our pillows, and honestly, I'm so tired from such a big night my eyes flutter shut. I can hear Paige and Trista whispering about something, but I'm too tired to care that I'm missing what they are saying.

"Everyone up!" I hear, as the lights flicker on and off. For a moment, I don't know where I am. I lift my head and look around. I'm on a chalky 4-inch mat at Perfect Balance.

"Up girls! It's 7 o'clock, classes start in an hour, all mats need to be put away!" she yells. She goes over to the stereo and turns on music, loud music. I hear girls groaning and grumbling.

"She's so mean. Remind me to change gyms before I have to train with her," Trista yawns.

"Did we even sleep at all?" Marissa asks. That is exactly how I feel. I feel like I just shut my eyes.

We drag ourselves out of our sleeping bags and start rolling them up. We are silent while we are doing this, which is unusual for this group. After we put our bags and pillows by the cubbies we start moving the mats back to their proper places in the gym; under the bars, under beams, and stacked by the stereo on floor. By the time this is done our parents start arriving to pick us up. My mom laughs when she sees my sleepy face and I shuffle to the car without even saying goodbye to my friends.

I ride home with my mom in silence. When we pull into the garage I see my dad loading the other car with skis. I say a sleepy hi to him and walk into the house. I can hear my brother's arguing about someone's missing gloves and someone else's missing socks.

"Your socks aren't missing Ethan; they're on the drying rack in the laundry room," my mom says.

"Why are they there? I thought Will took them," he says with exasperation.

"You're welcome for washing them," she says. Then she hands me a bagel and a banana and tells me to go up and take a nap.

"But I want to go skiing," I say, holding the banana and bagel.

"Baby Girl, look at you. You're exhausted.

You can't ski today."

"But I promise, I didn't stay up that late!" I lie.

"What's going on in here?" my dad asks, coming into the kitchen.

"Dad, tell her I can go skiing!" I plead.

"Sure, why not?" he says and I smile at my mom.

"*Mark!*" my mom says with a look at my dad.

"Oh, sorry, whatever your mom says," he amends.

"*Dad!*" I turn on him, "Why won't you guys let me ski? I love to ski and everyone is going without me!" Tears start forming in my eyes and falling down my face.

"Oh boy," my dad says, "I don't know what's going on here, but I'm going to round up the boys. You two figure it out," and he escapes upstairs.

"Why aren't you letting me do what everyone else gets to do?" I say to my mom through tears.

"Alexis, you're exhausted. You had your fun

and now it's time to sleep. You can ski another day." She takes my shoulders and turns me toward the stairs. I shuffled to my room in defeat and fall into bed.

Chapter 12

Split Leap on Beam

"Alexis, time to wake up," I hear my mom saying. I open my eyes and see Mom smiling down on me. I sit up and see that it is gray outside. "Baby girl, it's time for dinner, you need to get up."

"What?" I say, sitting up. "Dinner? How is it time for dinner? I just went to sleep."

"You've been sleeping all day. How late did you stay up anyway?" she asks.

I can't answer that question because my head is still reeling at the information that I slept all day. "All day?" I say quietly. My mom nods. "And the boys went skiing?" I ask, and my mom nods again. "I missed an entire Saturday?" I ask, tears welling up in my eyes. I don't know why, but this has me seriously upset. Tomorrow is Sunday, and Sunday is filled with church stuff, so I completely missed the best day of the week. And I missed skiing on top of it.

My mom doesn't seem the least bit upset, in fact, she is laughing. "Baby girl, it's a great lesson to learn at a young age. You can't stay up half the night and not pay the price the next day. Your body needs rest. This won't be the first time you'll try to squeeze more hours out of a day. It always catches up to you."

I look at my hands and think about what she is saying. "But when can I go skiing with dad? I keep missing it," I sulk.

"Hmm, I'm sure we can figure something out. But for now, I'll leave you to wake up while I finish making dinner. Come on down in the next 10 minutes or so, okay?" she says.

"Okay," I answer.

When I make my way down to dinner a few minutes later I can hear all my brothers talking at once about their epic ski day. I'm so jealous. I quietly sit down and eat my dinner and listen to them recount their jumps and crashes and favorite runs of the day.

Finally, my dad turns his attention to me, "How was your day, Alexis?"

"I slept through it," I pout.

"Welcome to the cruel reality of partying too hard," he says with a laugh. Why does everyone think this is so funny? My weekend has been stolen from me. "Tell me about the sleepover. What'd you do that kept you up so late?" he asks.

I tell him about the dance we made up for the talent show, about Katie's awesome gymnastics, and about the water fight.

"Well," he says when I finish, "all that sounds like it was worth a lost day."

"Are you girls ready for the talent show tryouts on Wednesday?" my mom asks.

"I think so, well, maybe we need to get together one more day," I confess.

"You don't have practice on Tuesday, why don't we invite your friends over Tuesday after school to practice one last time?"

"That would be good, thanks Mom," I say.

She smiles at me and then turns to my brothers, "We have been asked to sing at church tomorrow. I was thinking you kids could sing together."

My mom's suggestion is met with groans from my brothers.

"Mom, that's so lame," Ethan complains.

"Singing in church is an honor, and singing with your family is so sweet."

They all look down at their plates, trying to think of a way to weasel out of it.

"We don't have time to practice," Drew tries.

"You can practice tonight," she counters.

"Our voices don't sound good together," William fibs.

"They are beautiful together, and the church ward deserves to hear you!" she exclaims.

"Mom, we just don't want to. It's embarrassing. Why don't I just sing tomorrow?" Josh says, saving the rest of us.

My brothers look at Josh with relief. My mom surveys each of them and turns to me, "Do you want to sing with Josh?" she asks.

"Not really," I admit, which makes me feel bad.

"I can't believe this! I have the most talented kids. I have taught you to sing from the time you were toddlers, and no one will sing when we are asked to?" She pushes back from the table and stands up and starts clearing dishes in a huff.

We look at each other, not sure what to do short of having to sing, which no one wants to do.

"Let Josh do a solo," my dad says, "he'll be on his mission soon. He needs to learn to do things without his brothers."

My mom looks up and smiles. She is proud of my brother for choosing to go on a mission after he graduates high school. This makes her forget about the rest of us slackers.

"Do you think you need practice on your own hon?" she asks Josh.

He nods, she smiles, and we all smile. She nods, satisfied, and turns on the sink to rinse the dishes.

"You four owe me," Josh whispers under his breath.

"Sucker," Ethan whispers back.

Chapter 13

Hitch Kick Cartwheel on Floor

As soon as the bell rings for school to get out I run to the bathroom and change out of my uniform into leggings and a T-shirt for tryouts. My teammates and I decided that leggings would be best because we can do gymnastics in them.

As soon as I'm done changing I hustle over to the cafeteria at my school. I scan the room for my teammates and spot them along the far wall to the right of the stage. It's strange to see my teammates at Mountain View. I walk over to them and drop my backpack at my feet.

"Hey guys," I say.

"Alexis, your school is so much prettier than mine. It's brighter, ours is dark and gray everywhere," Trista comments. Trista goes to the local public school, Hilltop Elementary, with Savannah. I would trade bright colors for teammates that go to my school.

"Do they have a phone port?" Paige asks, holding up her phone which has the Katy Perry song on it.

"Mrs. Nelson said they would," I say looking around. I find the teacher in charge of the talent show talking with some parents. I should go over and ask her, but I'm shy and nervous. I know I need to be the one to take charge because I'm the one that goes to this school. But, for some reason, I can't move. It's weird having my girls here with me in charge. I'm never in charge.

Thankfully, Mrs. Smith walks to the stage at

the front of the room and loudly addresses all of us.

"Good Afternoon everyone. Look at this fantastic turn out for our Winter Wonderland Talent Show! As you know, these are tryouts. We must hold tryouts because we are committed to keeping the show to an hour and a half. We are also aiming to have a diverse show. We want to have as many different acts as possible. We have three teachers, three parents, and Principal Towers here to decide what acts make it into the show.

"I wish we could have all of you in the show, but we just can't. If your act is not chosen, it's because we are looking for a variety and exceptional talent. I encourage you to have fun today, enjoy watching your friends, and try again next year if you don't make it. Mrs. Nelson will tell you when you are up. You will be called up in the order we received your application," she concludes.

Yikes. Try again next year? Now I'm nervous.

Then Mrs. Nelson asks if we have any questions and I raise my hand and ask about the phone port. She says one of the parents will show me. A parent quietly walks over to us and Paige follows her over to the receiver and shows the volunteer which song it is and the she assures Paige she will turn it on when it's our turn.

Then the tryouts begin and we sit down to watch. First there is a boy who does a karate routine. He is really good. He even does some gymnastics, but with bad form. I think he meant for his feet to be flexed and his head out on his skills. It was weird and cool at the same time.

Next a girl plays the piano, then a violinist, and after that a singer. While we are watching the singer a volunteer mom comes over to us and says we are after the next act and to start getting ready. I nod to her and look at my teammates. I whisper to them that we are up after the next act.

We get up and start walking to the side of the stage. The singer finishes and a dancing group files on stage. They are in matching red sparkling tank tops and black workout shorts with a sparkly red stripe down the side. They have on little black shoes and have matching pony tails with red ribbons. My heart sinks. They look great. How did they coordinate all of that so fast? I turn to look at Paige with wide eyes, and she is as shocked as I am. The music comes on, it's "Timber" by Ke$ha and Pit Bull. Good thing we didn't go with that song. We would be cut for sure for being too similar.

We all quietly watch them and they look great. All their moves are perfect, together, and cool. But the hardest thing they do is a split leap; that makes me feel better. They smile at the judges and look like they have been on stage many times. I know the girls. They are the popular girls in the 4th grade. They always eat lunch together and play 4-square with the boys. I realize now that they probably see each other a lot outside of school.

Their amazing performance ends and

unfortunately, it's our turn. I look at my teammates and we all stand up and walk to the stage. We look like a hodge-podge mess compared to those Timber girls. We are wearing different colored legging and a fitted tank top or T-shirt. We thought to wear leggings, but beyond that we didn't think to coordinate our clothing. Why didn't we? We could have worn our matching PBGA workout leotards.

I feel so rag tag as we take our positions on the stage. Our Katy Perry song starts and we start our roll off. As soon as the dance begins I forget about our clothing and enjoy the dance, the tumbling, the energy. We have practiced this a ton of times and it's fun on the stage with my friends. I hear some of the kids clap for Trista as she does her back tuck at the end. When the music ends we hold our pose for three seconds like Katie told us to.

I have a huge grin on my face and I'm breathing hard in and out as I hold my hand over my head in our ending pose.

"Very nice, girls," I hear Mrs. Nelson say. We come out of our pose and walk off stage.

"Great back handsprings, Trista," I hear Marissa say. "Your form was awesome and they were so long, you almost went off the stage."

Trista laughs, "I know! I could have done one more, but I ran out of room."

I can tell my teammates had fun and are pumped up about our performance.

"Alexis?" Mrs. Nelson says to me. I stop and turn toward her. My teammates keep chatting and walking back to where we were sitting before.

I look at Mrs. Nelson as she comes up to me. "Whose class are your friends in? You didn't list it on your talent show application."

"Oh, they don't go here," I explain.

"None of them?" she asks.

"No,"

"How do you know your friends?" she asks.

"We go to the same gymnastics club together," I explain.

"What school do they go to?" she asks.

"They go to Hilltop, Aspen, and St. Mary's."

"I see," she says making a note on her clip board. "Okay, thanks Alexis," she says, dismissing me. I turn and go back to my friends. They're still chattering about how our dance went. The next group is up and we are told by one of the teachers to quiet down, so we do. We watch the next group, which is singing and dancing. They are good too, although not as good at the Timber dance routine.

"It may be tougher than I thought to make this talent show," I whisper to Marissa.

Marissa nods, "We have some serious competition," she whispers back. "But so far we are the only routine that has gymnastics in it. That will help because they said they want a variety."

By the time my mom comes to pick us up we are all arguing about who will make the talent show.

"The karate guy, for sure," Trista says, "He was really good. Do you know him Alexis?" she asks me.

"Sort of, he's a fifth grader, so not that well."

"I liked the girl who sang that Adele song by herself. I didn't know kids our size could sing like that," Marissa chimes in.

"Hi girls," my mom greets us as we pile into her van. "How'd it go?"

"Ours was the best," Trista says with confidence. "No one else did gymnastics," she says smugly.

"But that other dancing group was amazing," Paige points out. "The one that danced to 'Timber,'" she reminds us. "Glad we didn't pick the same song at least."

"Well, I'm proud of you guys for putting something together and doing it," my mom says pulling away from the curb. "Remember if they don't pick you guys it doesn't always have anything to do with you. They can't have too much of one type of performance. And they are trying to keep it under two hours."

"We know, they told us," Savannah answers.

"They'll pick us," Trista says again, "our dance may not have been as good as the Timber girls, but we had gymnastics in our routine, and that makes it so much cooler."

We all start talking at once again about who we thought was the best and who we thought the teachers liked the best. Before we know it my mom is pulling up to PBGA to drop us off at practice. We pile out and head upstairs to the bathrooms to change and then back down to the cubbies in the lobby. We are still talking about the tryouts when James tells us to stop acting like gossipy old ladies and to go do our warm up laps on the floor.

By the end of workout I feel great and I know Trista is right. We are totally going to make it in the talent show.

Chapter 14

Sissonne on Floor

"What do you mean we can't be in the show?" I yell. "We're the best performance! Did those red girls take the only dancing spot? Because we are more than just dancing."

"Not exactly," My mom says. "Baby girl, calm down so I can explain." I start pacing the kitchen,

what am I going to tell my friends? They worked
so hard on the dance.

"I got a call from Mountain View. They loved
your performance and were really impressed.
However, this is a school talent show and you are
the only one that goes to Mountain View. They
asked if you could just do it on your own."

"No, I can't do it on my own. It's made for
five people. There's roll offs and different timing
for different passes, and I can't do all the skills
Trista does."

"Can you change it a little? They really liked
the idea of dance and gymnastics."

"Why can't my friends be in it? This is so unfair.
The red girls get to dance with all of their friends,
why can't I?" I moan.

"I'm sure all those girls go to Mountain View,"
my mom says in an annoyingly calm voice.

"This is so unfair!" I yell at my mom, "Can you
talk to them?" I plead.

"Baby, I tried," she says and comes over to
give me a hug, but I don't want a hug. I run past

her and up to my room.

Once in my room I'm not sure what to do. So I start kicking stuffed animals, which doesn't help. I pick up and throw a few of them, which still doesn't help. I plop on the floor with my legs crossed. I prop my elbows on my knees and bury my head in my hands.

I stay that way, wondering what is worse: having to tell my teammates they can't be in the show, or doing the show alone. I don't want to do the show alone. From the very beginning I didn't want to do it alone.

I hear a knock at my door, "What!?" I holler.

"It's Drew," I hear Drew say from the other side if the door. I am silent for a few seconds before I tell him he can come in.

"Hey," Drew says as he walks in my room. He surveys the stuffed animals laying all over the floor. "Why does your room look like Will's?" he asks.

"Because I felt like throwing something, okay?" I respond in a nasty tone, even though he's not the one who deserves the tone. The dumb talent show people at my school do.

"Okay," he says, and sits down next to me. "Why did Mom send me up here?" he asks.

"Maybe so I have someone real to punch?"

"Lex, what happened?" he asks.

I look up from my hands into his face, "After all that work we can't be in the talent show because my teammates don't go to Mountain View."

"But I heard Mom say you could still be in the show."

"By myself," I moan and fall back onto my back with my knees up. Drew frowns and looks at me for a moment.

"What's wrong with that?" he asks.

"I don't want to do it by myself. Besides being scary, it's kind of lame and not as fun as a group thing," I confess.

"Well, maybe I could do something with you. I go to Mountain View and I can do gymnastics," he says giving me his lop sided grin.

"But you don't want to do a girly dance routine."

"No, I don't want to do a girly dance routine. Think of something else then Lex. What else could we do?"

I prop myself up on my elbows, "I don't know," I mumble.

"Well, I'm up for doing something with you, if it's cool," he says and stands up. "But, I don't dance to Katy Perry," he qualifies. "I'll go tell Mom you're fine, just being whiney about the whole thing."

"Drew!" I yell, and pick up a stuffed purple kitten to throw at him. He scampers out of the room, slamming the door behind him, making the kitten hit the door.

What would I do with Drew? A bunch of tumbling passes without music? Lame. And he was probably just being nice anyway. He never wanted to do the talent show in the first place.

Think, Lexi, think. What can I do? I need Marissa, she's a good thinker. That's it, Marissa! I jump up and run down to my mom.

"Can Marissa come over?" I blurt out.

"You just spent two hours together," my mom points out.

"Yeah, but that was before I knew about the talent show problem," I explain.

"It's almost dinnertime."

"After dinner?" I beg.

"Oh, alright. I'll text her mom."

"Have you told the others?" Marissa asks.

"No," I say pacing my room. Marissa's mom dropped her off after dinner and now she is sitting on my bed, crossed legged, and looking at me. Her long black hair is hanging well past her shoulders and she almost looks like a different person to me with her hair down. We only have an hour before my mom is returning her home, since it's already late.

"You should tell them," she presses.

"I *know*," I snap, throwing my hands up. I immediately feel bad for getting sassy with Marissa. But she ignores me and continues talking.

"Why don't you do the dance on your own? I bet Paige will help you re-choreograph it to get rid of the roll offs and extra tumbling," she offers.

I shake my head, no, and continue pacing. What am I going to do? Not do the talent show at all?

"Can you tell them no?" Marissa asks me.

"What?"

"Can you tell the talent show people that you just don't want to do it anymore?"

Not do it? "Well, yeah, I guess. But I want to do it, just not by myself," I admit.

"Why?" Marissa asks.

I stop pacing and sit down on my bed and face Marissa, "I guess I wanted to make my mom proud. She loves performances. I don't really like plays. My mom used to take me to auditions and I would never get the part. The talent show seemed like a fun easy performance I could actually do. I can do gymnastics so much better than memorize lines. And she was so happy when I said we were trying out," I admit.

Marissa thinks about this and says, "Alright then, no saying no. Do you have any friends at school you could teach the dance to?" Marissa asks.

"I know a bunch of kids from church that go to Mountain View, but I don't know if they can dance. I'm so lame. How do I not know one other girl who can dance?"

"You're not lame. We're all like that. It's called being a 'gym rat,'" she says smiling.

"Savannah's not, I always hear her talking about her school friends," I say.

"Savannah's an only child. School friends are more important to her."

"Yeah, I guess. But being the only girl is like being an only child," I say.

"No it's not," Marissa disagrees, not allowing me to feel sorry for myself. "Think about it. You hang out with Drew all the time. You guys talk about gymnastics and whatever else. Savannah doesn't have that."

"I guess not," I agree sullenly.

"Does he play on the bars at recess too?" she asks.

"Drew?" I ask and she nods, "Sometimes," I admit.

"Then you have school friends, your brothers," she says smiling.

"My brothers," I repeat. Great. My only friends are my silly, rowdy, stinky, brothers.

Then it hits me, my brothers can sing. They used to sing in church all the time. My head snaps up and I yell, "That's it! My brothers!"

"Your brothers?" Marissa asks confused, "I thought Drew was the only one that could tumble."

"He is, but the rest can sing! I can't believe I didn't think of this before, they are amazing singers."

I jump off the bed and go tearing out of my room.

"Drew! Drew!" I yell. I run to his room and almost run into him as he opens the door and sticks his head out.

"What? Are you okay?"

"I'm fine, you need to do the talent show with me!"

"I told you I would do it with you. But I'm not dancing to Katie Perry."

"No Katie Perry, something else. Singing. And I need Josh, Ethan, and Will too!" I squeal. Drew starts laughing. "What's so funny?"

"You might have a prayer getting me to do something with you, but you won't get those guys to get on a stage with you. They won't even sing in church for Mom anymore."

"Wanna bet?" I say turning my blue eyes up to him in a perfect pout.

"That only works with Mom and Dad," he says, referring to my pout. I stop my silly look and

cross my arms over my chest and glare at him.
"Good luck, let me know how it turns out," he
says and shuts the door in my face.

.

Chapter 15

Front Handspring on Floor

I spin on my heel and this time almost run into Marissa who is standing right behind me.

"If you don't have him in your corner, I don't

know how you're going to get the others to agree," Marissa accurately points out. But I'm not going to give up. *Think, think, how can I get them to agree.*

"MOM!" I yell running down the stairs with Marissa on my heels.

When I find my mom, I quickly tell her my idea of having my brothers join me in the talent show. She, of course, loves the idea, but isn't much more helpful than Drew.

"How are you going to convince them to do it?" she asks, emptying the dishwasher and putting water glasses away.

"I thought you could," I say weakly.

"I'm not going to play the Mom-card for something like this. I save that for homework, church, and curfew," she replies, walking back and picking up more dishes.

"But mo-u-m," I whine.

"I do think it would be really cute if you all did something together, but it's going to be a tough sell."

I stick my lip out and look down. She's right. How can I possibly convince them?

"I'll tell you what, tomorrow after dinner we should have everyone home from sports by 6:30 or 7. We can hold a family meeting and you can talk to the boys. They will all be here."

"What about the talent show people?" I ask.

"I'll call and tell them you need one more day to decide what to do. You need to figure out how to convince your brothers," she says pulling out the silverware tray. "Here, finish this. I have to go pick up Ethan. Josh is here and so is Drew. When I get back I'll take Marissa home, so be ready in about 15," she says, grabbing her keys and walking out the door.

I start putting silverware away in the silverware drawer and I think about what my mom said. I have to convince my brothers. Marissa sits up at the counter across from me.

"How are you going to convince them?" she asks.

"I don't know," I say stacking forks.

"You know them better than me. What do boys like?"

"I don't know. Ever since they grew out of Legos I'm not so sure anymore. They are always at sports, or listening to music, or playing on their phones," I say with a frustrated sigh. "They seem pretty obsessed with cars and movies where things blow up," I add.

"Hmm, maybe you could bribe them with movies or music," she suggests.

"How am I going to do that? I have no money. I don't babysit yet. I only have Christmas money."

"Christmas money works," she says.

I really don't want to use Christmas money. "Can't I just explain to them it will be cool?" I ask and I see Marissa is biting her lip thinking about this.

"How is it cool for them?" she asks.

"I don't know! They're weird teenage boys. How should I know?" I wail.

"Call Paige."

"What?" I ask.

"Call Paige," she repeats. "She might know about teenage boys because she's almost a teenager. Let's ask her."

We use Marissa's phone to call her (because I don't have one yet).

"Hey Marissa," Paige answers.

"It's actually Alexis," I say.

"Oh, what's up?" Paige asks and I can tell she's confused. Probably since I never call her.

"Hey, I have bad news," I blurt out. Paige is silent so I continue. "we didn't make the talent show."

"Wow, really? That stinks. I thought we were good."

"Well it's not that we weren't good, it's that I guess all the kids in the show are supposed to be from Mountain View," I explain.

"That's stupid, you're from Mountain View, isn't that enough?"

"Guess not," I sulk.

"Are you still going to do it? On your own?"

she asks.

"I think I'm going to still try to be in the show, but with my brothers."

"Your brothers? What talent do they have? I thought they did basketball."

"They can sing, they just don't like to very often. I need to convince them to do this with me," I explain.

"Okay," Paige says, confused.

"I'm calling to ask you what boys like. I need to bribe them to be in the show with me," I admit.

I hear Paige chuckle and then say, "I only have a little brother. I don't know what boys like."

"But you're my brothers' age, sort of. What do boys at your school like? What do teenage boys like?" I ask.

"Well . . . they like showing off by throwing the football really far. And they like bragging and teasing each other," she thinks out loud.

"Why do they show off?" Marissa asks

"For girls mostly," Paige says.

"That's it!" Marissa says.

"You're right! Why didn't I think of it sooner?" Paige exclaims.

"What? What am I missing here?" I say, confused.

"They like girls," Paige explains to me. "Tell them girls will be at the show and that girls will think they're cute for doing a performance with their little sister. Plus, guys in a band are cool, all guys want to be rock stars. They can pretend to be rock stars and feel cool and be cool and girls will love it."

"Girls?" I repeat. "But I'm a girl and they don't show off for me."

"You're not a girl they want to kiss," she qualifies. Good point. Girls it is then. I'll promise them girls at the show. *Where do I get girls?*

"Hey, Paige?" I ask. "Will you come to the show?" *There's one.*

"Yeah, I'll be there. I have to go okay?" and we disconnect. I look at Marissa.

She looks back at me and shrugs, "She has a point. Use that angle and you won't even have to use your Christmas money."

Chapter 16

Back Walkover on Floor

"I'll do it if you do my chores for a week," Ethan says, the jerk.

I'm standing in front of my brothers. We're down in the basement after dinner. My mom sent all of us down here to talk together, she knew I was going to try to convince them to do this with me. But I'm not sure she knew how hard it was going to be.

"Ethan, I said girls would be there, I didn't say anything about chores," I clarify.

"Chores for a week," he stubbornly replies. I nod and he leans back on the couch and crosses his arms to see what the others will do.

"I don't go to Mountain View anymore. Why do you think they'll let me do it if they won't let your teammates do it?" Josh asks. He's right, Josh goes to Snowcap Canyon High School.

"Since the rest of us go to Mountain View, Mom thought they'd make an exception for family," I answer. Mountain View has kids from kindergarten through eighth grade, so all of us except for Josh go to school there.

"Find out first before I waste my time down here," he says.

"So you'll do it?" I ask, clapping my hands together.

Josh shrugs and says, "If you make sure I can be in it, sure, why not?"

"You promise girls will be there?" Will asks.

"I promise! I'll invite them myself. And I'll have

Mom record it and put it on You Tube so all your friends can see it."

"Let's only post it if it looks good, it might be a bust," Ethan says.

"It's not going to be a bust," Drew says standing up and walking over to the speaker and turning it on. Then he taps a few buttons on his phone and One Direction starts singing *What Makes You Beautiful*. "We should sing to this, it has a range we can do," he says with a grin.

We quietly listen to the song. I can tell my brothers are listening and considering how this song would work for us.

The song blares out from teenage male voices:

"The words aren't quite right Drew," Josh interrupts. Drew pauses the song.

"Then we change it," he says simply. "We can get the karaoke version of this song and sing it the way we want to."

"How would you change it?" Ethan asks.

"Like when they sing about the girl flipping

her hair maybe we say something about an actual flip and she does a flip. Or when it says stuff about wanting the girl we say something about loving the girl.

"Eew," Ethan says making a gagging gesture.

"Seriously Eth, we love her, she's our sister, but we don't want her, like, for a girlfriend or anything."

"Those changes would work. Let's try it," Josh says standing up.

In that moment I know they are in. Once Josh is standing and ready to go, I know all my brothers will agree.

Two hours later we are ready to sing it on our own. Josh took Liam's lines, Ethan took Harry's lines, and William and Drew are to join in on the chorus. They are looking at the words on Josh and William's phones. We changed the lines just how Drew had recommended. I will not be singing, my part is to dance around them and do a back handspring when they boys sing the sentence about a flip. And to smile when they sing about me smiling.

"Yeah, let's try it," Ethan says, and I'm glad he is finally going along with the performance. I hope he has forgotten about making me do a week of his chores. "I have the karaoke version downloaded," he says and looks up, "You guys ready?" We all nod and he pushes play on his phone and sets it down. The song starts playing through the Bluetooth speaker Drew brought down from his room.

We stand looking at each other, listening to the first bars of the song and trying to listen for when to start singing. Then Josh starts at just the right time. He sounds just like the real singer. Then he smiles a huge smile at me and I start walking in a strut to the front of the group. My brothers all start laughing and then they jump in for the chorus.

We practice the song several more times until all the boys know their lines and I know exactly where to walk between them, when to tumble, and when to smile up at Josh, which they all decided would be super cute at the end.

"I'm beat! I think we've got it. Can I go?"
Ethan asks.

"Let's show Mom," Drew says excitedly.

"I think we should surprise Mom at the show,"
Josh says. "What do you think, Alexis?" They all
look at me for my answer.

I'm not sure what to say at first. My brothers
never look to me for an answer. "Surprise her,
and all of our friends. It should a secret," I decide
with a grin.

"Can I go?" Ethan persists.

"We have to do it one more time so we can
record it and e-mail it to the talent show people.
They still have to decide if we are good enough
to be in the show," I explain.

"Ugh, one more time, so make it good."

"Who's going to record it if Mom's not
allowed to see it?" William asks.

"I bet dad's home," I say and run up the stairs
to see if my dad is home. I find him in the kitchen
talking with my Mom.

"Hey Baby Girl, did the boys agree?" my mom asks me.

"Yes, but I need Dad to record it for us and send it to the talent show people," I explain.

"I'll do it!" she says eagerly.

"No, we want Dad to do it," I say. My dad grins and my mom looks a little hurt. "It's a surprise for you," I explain to my mom. "You're not allowed to see it until the show. If we get in the show."

"Awesome, let's do this," my dad says walking toward the basement door and pulling out his phone.

We do a pretty good job on the first try and my dad gets a decent video. I think we can do better, but my brothers are dying to be done.

"Are we done yet?" Ethan whines.

"Yes, but meet back here tomorrow before dinner. We'll practice it every night this week until it's awesome," Josh says. He winks at me and heads up the stairs. In that moment I feel so lucky to have brothers. I can't wait to show this performance to my mom. She is going to be floored.

I head upstairs with my dad and we talk to my mom about my choice to do the show with my brothers. She calls the volunteer in charge of the show and tells her I still want to be in the show but with my brothers. My mom explains that Josh does not go to Mountain View, but that he did when he was younger.

She finally gets off the phone with a grin, "Send your video to this email. She'll let you know by tomorrow if you're in."

I grab the slip of paper she is handing me and my dad helps me get into his email and send the video over to the woman in charge of the show.

Chapter 17

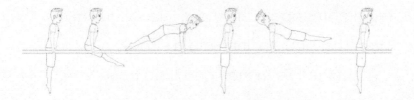

Tap Swings on Parallel Bars

"Have you told your teammates they got cut?" Drew asks. We are riding in the car on our way to gymnastics practice.

"They didn't get cut; they just can't be in it," I say.

"Same thing."

"It is not. Our dance was awesome and we

would've totally made it if it weren't for the lame rule about Mountain View kids."

Drew shrugs in response to me and after a moment he says, "Our act might be better."

"It might," I agree.

We get to practice a few minutes early. Drew immediately goes out into the training area and finds his teammate, Aaron. I hang around the cubbies in the lobby for a moment to tell my teammates about the show. I slowly stuff my sweatshirt and flip flops into a cubby.

Just then Savannah and Trista bounce in.

"Hey Lex, we were just talking about you."

"Yeah?" I say, not sure what else to say.

"Yeah," Trista says. "We were talking about how we could practice the dance again this Friday at PNO before the dress rehearsal next week."

"Um, about that," I mumble.

"Do you think we should get together Saturday too, so we have two practices before the dress rehearsal?" Savannah chimes in.

"You guys, I have to tell you something," I finally say.

"What?" Trista says stuffing her hoodie into a cubby.

"Well, we can't be in the show."

"We didn't make it?" Trista yells. "That's impossible! We were the only gymnastics group and the second best dancing group!"

"You're right,"

"Then why aren't we in it?" she screeches.

"Trista, pipe down," Katie says from behind the front desk.

"Why didn't we make it?" she whispers, which makes Savannah and I giggle.

That's when Marissa walks in with Paige right behind her.

"We didn't make the talent show!" Trista yells over to them.

"Seriously Trista, I'm going to send you out to do push-ups," Katie says.

"Sorry, sorry," she says, and we are quiet for a moment.

"We know," Paige says.

"You know!" Trista yells and slaps her hand over her mouth.

"Go do 20," Katie says without looking away from the credit card she is running for a parent enrolling their child in classes.

"Fine, come tell me what's going on while I do push-ups," Trista says and we follow her out into the gym.

We go to the end of the tumble track and sit down. It is the only corner of the gym not being used.

Trista starts doing her push-ups and the rest of us sit down.

"What happened?" Savannah asks, wide eyed.

"My school only wanted kids who go to Mountain View to be in the show," I finally explain.

"That is so unfair! You go there!" Trista says from her push-up position.

"I know, it totally stinks, I'm sad you guys

won't be doing it with me."

"Are you doing it by yourself?" Savannah asks.

"No, I'm going to do it with my brothers."

"Drew too?" Trista asks, taking a break and sitting on her knees.

"All of them. But I want you guys to be there. Can you guys come and watch?" I ask.

"What about our dance?" Savannah says, "We worked so hard on it."

"We could still do our dance," Marissa says.

"You just heard her, we're not allowed," Trista says.

"We can do it here on Friday at PNO. I've been thinking about it and I think we should do our dance in our PBGA workout leotards and record it so we always have it," Marissa explains.

"That's a really good idea," Paige says.

"I'm in, and I'll be at your show," Trista says getting back into a push up position for the rest of her punishment.

"What is all this sitting around," James says

walking up.

"We're keeping Trista company while she does push-ups," I explain.

"Too loud in the lobby again, huh Triss?"

Trista doesn't say anything and James chuckles.

"You four go run your laps. Trista, join them when you're done.

Drew and I are late for PNO because Ethan and William decided to join us at the last minute. I quickly stuff my sweatshirt into a cubby and run into the gym. Sure enough, all my teammates are there wearing their PBGA workout leotards. They are over by the pit building a foam block wall to run and jump over and land in the pit.

"You all remembered," I say smiling.

"Of course we remembered," Marissa says.

"Do you have the music?" Trista asks me. I nod with a grin.

"Should we practice once? And who is recording us?" Paige asks.

"Drew said he would. He has Will's phone," I answer. Seriously, Drew and I should get phones soon. I don't know why Ethan and Will get phones. We're more responsible than them.

We abandon the foam wall where it is. We know other kids will use it. We practice the routine once through and call Drew over. He sits with his back to the mirror and is ready to record us.

We get in our starting pose and the music begins. We have done the dance so many times, it's fun to perform it for a camera. And even though we didn't really warm up, everyone's tumbling in the dance is really strong. When the song finally ends, we all remember to hold our ending pose.

We can see Drew touch the screen and lower the phone.

"That was really good. I mean it. It's too bad you can't do it for the talent show," he says with genuine disappointment.

"Can we see it?" Trista says bouncing up to Drew and looking over his shoulder as he holds up the phone to show her. We crowd around Drew and watch it once through.

"The roll off looks cool," Marissa says as we watch the dance begin.

"It is good choreography, Paige," Savannah says.

"Holy cow, my legs really are super bent on my leaps, I thought James was exaggerating," Trista says and we all laugh.

The rest of the viewing goes like this. We enjoy watching the dance and are critical of our gymnastics. It's fun and weird to see ourselves on video.

Just as the song is ending Katie walks up, "What have you guys got there?" she asks us. We show her the video. "That's really cute, can I put it on the PBGA Facebook page?"

We all agree and she says she'll send a text to our parents asking permission for us to be on the Facebook page.

"Great idea, Marissa," I say, "I'm so glad we were able to perform it one last time and keep it forever."

"No problem," she says, "it seemed like such a waste not to even get it on video." I nod in agreement and go to put William's phone in my cubby. When I come back my teammates are back to building a new wall. The last one got kicked over.

Two hours later Josh shows up to pick us up. "Why are you so early?" Drew asks.

"Mom just said to come get you on my way home. I'm on my way home, so let's go."

I head over to get Ethan and William who are swinging on the rope.

"Is that your oldest brother?" Savannah asks.

"Yeah. We have to go," I answer.

"Is he singing with you too?"

"Yeah, Ethan, William! Josh is here!" I yell over

to them.

"You should show us your performance," Savannah continues.

"What?" I say, turning to her.

"I'd love to see whatever it is you are doing with your brothers," she says.

I look back at Josh standing in the doorway of the training area. Great idea!

"Hey Josh," I skip over to him. "Let's practice our song once here!"

"We can practice at home tomorrow or something," he says.

"But we'll be skiing tomorrow and church stuff Sunday, we may not have another chance until the dress rehearsal," I point out.

"I guess we could count this as our last practice. We are all here and I have the music on my phone," he says without much enthusiasm.

"It would be lame to sing here," Ethan says from behind me. As soon as I hear Ethan say he thinks it is a bad idea, I know Josh will be up for it.

"It's a good idea, Ethan. There's a ton of kids

we can practice in front of," Josh says.

I jump and clap my hands, "This will be great!" Now Katie, Melony, and James will get to see my other act!

We don't have microphones, but our mom has taught us how to project our voices. Josh plugs in his phone into the gym receiver and shows Paige which song to play. We decide to sing on the floor and face the tumble track. James gathers up the kids to sit on the tumble track for our song.

The karaoke track starts and my brothers begin singing at each of their parts. The song is even more fun to perform with more space than we've had in the basement. I'm so proud of my brothers and I'm having so much fun. The kids in the gym are captivated, even the little ones. And when we finish they all clap for us.

We are better than I thought. This is going to be the best act ever!

.

Chapter 18

Standing Back Handspring on Floor

This is going to be the worse act ever! Josh is not here, Ethan keeps acting like he can't remember his lines and Drew is out talking to my teammates instead of back stage with me. What he is doing? Where's Josh? Where is our music? Where are the microphones?

"Ethan, do you have the music?"

"I forgot it," he says with a grin

"Ethan!"

"Relax stress case, I have it. I already gave it to the audio people," then he looks over my shoulder and says, "Hey."

I hear Paige behind me give a shy, "Hey," back.

"Paige! You're here! I'm so glad you made it," I say, turning around and giving her a hug.

"Is it going to be as good as my dance?" she asks teasingly.

"Nope, but it was the best I could come up with without you," I say.

"Good, you look great," she says taking in my PBGA leotard and black hot pants. "Do you want some light make-up?" she asks.

"Make-up?" I say. Would my mom kill me? Her Baby Girl wearing make-up?

"Just so we can see your face in the bright lights, it's not like you're wearing make up to school or anything," she justifies.

"Okay", I agree. Paige moves me over to a stool and pulls little compacts and brushes out of her bag. As I let her add blush to my face, I can't stop worrying, where is Josh?

"Relax," Paige orders. "Man, why are you so nervous? You don't get this nervous for meets," she points out. "Except maybe on beam," she amends.

"I know," I sigh. "I guess because I know what to expect at meets. I don't have to count on my brothers. And my mom knows what happens in a meet, this is a surprise for her and I want it to be great. I'm never the one that does something great for my mom. Plus, I've never done anything in front of my classmates before."

"It will be great."

"What if Josh doesn't get here?"

"He'll be here, and if your show is a surprise for your mom, anything you do will seem great. She doesn't know how you practiced it. If you mess up just smile and keep going." I heave a huge sigh, she's right, but I still have a nauseous stomach, how do people do this? I'm so glad I never got any of those roles my mom took me to audition for.

"Close your eyes," she says. I close my eyes and she brushes eye shadow on my eyelids.

"Is this how you feel before meets?" I ask.

"Not really. I think you're right, it's harder in front of classmates."

"Gee, thanks," I say.

"Open," I open my eyes to Paige giving me a critical look. Then she rummages through her bag and pulls out lip gloss. "You're welcome. Now this is light and will just give you the perfect amount of shimmer, pucker up," I do as she says and she applies the lip gloss.

"When are you up?" Paige asks.

"Last. They put us last after they saw us in the dress rehearsal," I reply.

"Wow, you guys must be the best act if they're putting you last," she says and this comment makes me even more nervous, but I just nod.

"Looks great," I hear Josh say as he walks up.

"You're here!" I say jumping up.

"Of course I'm here," he says and puts his hands in his pockets. "Mom would've killed me if I disappointed the Baby Girl."

"Josh!" I say embarrassed he used my family nick name in front of Paige. But she just drops the lip gloss in her bag without a word and zips it up.

"I'm going to go back my seat," Paige informs me. "We're on the front left. Break a leg."

"I'm here in plenty of time," Josh continues.

"No you're not, the show starts any second."

"We're the last act, worry wart," he says, sauntering off. I swear, keeping my brothers all in one place and accounted for is impossible.

Once the talent show starts and I watch the other acts from back stage I become less nervous. None of the other acts are nearly as fun as ours and the audience seems to love them anyway. I peek out at the audience and I see my teammates on the front left just like Paige said and my parents right next to them, more toward the middle. My mom seems to be enjoying herself. That's good. She was not happy we wouldn't let her see our act. We've been practicing every night after dinner and we never once let my mom down to the basement to see it. Although, maybe she heard it, now that I think about it.

I look back to the stage and I see the violinist walking off stage and the principal is introducing the dance performance that goes right before us. Oh, gosh, we are next. As my panic sets in my brothers start materializing around me from out of nowhere. I take a good look at them. They are so handsome, they almost look like the boy band, One Direction. Josh, William, and Ethan are all in jeans and graphic T-shirts, 'trendy but not trying too hard' is what Josh instructed. Drew and I are in our blue and white PBGA workout clothes because we will both be tumbling.

"Where have you guys been?" I whisper.

"Drew's been flirting with your teammates," Ethan supplies. What? I look at Drew. He shrugs unhelpfully and gives me his grin.

"Music is queued up?" Josh asks Ethan, Ethan

nods.

"Lights? Did you talk to the lights guy?" Josh asks William.

"Yep, we're good, stop being such a mom."

"Just making sure you knuckleheads did what I asked you to do," Josh fires back. The red Ke$ha dance comes to an end and the crowd is clapping furiously.

"They liked them," Drew comments.

"We're better," Josh says, as the principle walks out to introduce us.

.

Chapter 19

Mountain View Talent Show

"The next act is my favorite kind, a family act. A family of five, four of which go to Mountain View Charter School and we had to make a special exception for the oldest brother, and alumni of Mountain View, and is now a sophomore at Snowcap Canyon High School. Let's give a huge round of applause for our last performance of the evening, the Bingham Kids," she yells and I hear the music start.

As the music begins Josh saunters out with the mic and starts signing the first four lines of the song.

Then Ethan wonders onto the stage singing the next two lines.

Ethan is followed by William and Drew. They all start signing the chorus and I run and do a round off and two back handsprings in front of them.

Then I run behind them and walk to the middle of them and act shy and smile as they sing.

Then I skip between them to get ready for another pass.

Then we line up with me in the middle, two of my brothers on each side, and we do a dance step together as William sings his four lines.

My brothers sound great, they sound just like One Direction.

Then Josh steps forward for two more of Harry's lines.

Then the chorus repeats itself, all four boys are signing and I do my tumbling and skipping between them again.

We get to the end of the song and as the boys start signing the last chorus they put their hands over their heads and clap.

Then Josh yells, "C'mon y'all, get on your feet and help us out!"

We are dancing and clapping with our hands over our heads I see the audience standing up and clapping too! So amazing! I can see my mom in front, on her feet, clapping, with tears in her eyes. I give her a huge grin and turn to Josh for our last part of the song.

Josh gets down on one knee and grabs my hand and sings to me his last five solo lines.

Then he gets up and they sing the chorus one

more time. And rather than me tumbling across the stage like I did during the other choruses, Drew gives his mic to Ethan and we both do back handsprings across the front of the stage. The crowd loves this new twist of him joining me.

The audience is on their feet clapping, singing, the music is perfect and fun, this is fantastic!

We line up across the stage one more time for the last two lines of the song and they all sing together,

We punch the air three times with the last three beats. We hold our ending rock star pose with our right arms over our head in a fist. The music stops and all we can hear is clapping.

The spot light on us shuts off and it's dark. We drop our hands and look at each other.

"Well that kicked butt," Josh whispers. Then the lights come back on and the other kids in the talent show file on stage. They line up in front of us and each group bows. Then the kids line up behind us and we walk forward holding hands and the five of us hold hands and take a bow and the clapping gets louder for us and there is even whistling. The red curtain drops and everyone starts talking at once.

"I didn't know you guys could sing that well,"

"– did you see, we got the entire crowd on their feet –"

"– those flips were so cool, can you teach me to do that?"

Then principal Towers comes over and quiets us down. "We are going to pull up the curtain one more time to thank the volunteers of the show. You guys stay how you are," she says to us. The curtain comes up, and the two volunteers and teachers come forward and Principal Towers thanks them for putting together the show and gives them flowers. The curtain falls again and we start chatting again now that we are safely behind the curtain.

"Great show tonight! You guys can go see your parents now," she says, herding us off stage.

We file off stage with everyone still talking at

once and my brothers are so happy with themselves.

We find our mom waiting for us at the edge of the stage. She is crying and laughing and hugging everyone. After she hugs all my brothers she grabs me, "Baby Girl, you did what I have been trying to do for years and could never accomplish."

She squeezes me tight and I look up at her, "Really? What did I do?"

"You got your brothers to sing together! I've always known they were great singers and that their voices sound amazing together. You five stole the show," she says letting me go.

"They are really good," I hear Paige say. I look around and see my teammates are all there, beaming at me.

"You all made it!" I exclaim.

"Of course we made it, we wouldn't have missed it," Savannah adds.

"I'm sorry our dance wasn't in it," I say to the group, and I mean it, even though I had a great time with my brothers.

"It's okay, what you guys did was better anyway," Marissa adds matter-of-factly.

"Yeah, who knew your brothers were so talented?" Trista says.

That makes me smile a huge smile. Like my mom, I knew.

"I guess we all learned something," I say with a grin.

"What?" They all ask.

"Brothers have talent, too!" I answer.

The Kip

Chapter 1

"For warms-ups today I want you to go to bars and work kips until I get there," James instructs.

We nod at him as we stuff our sweatshirts into a cubby in the lobby of Perfect Balance Gymnastics Academy.

It's my first day of Level 4 gymnastics practice. My teammates and I finished our Level 3 competition season last fall. In January, we had our awards banquet where we found out that we all moved up to Level 4. Moving up means we get to work out three days a week instead of just two. Even though we knew we were going to be Level 4s, our training schedule didn't change until now. Katie, the owner of Perfect Balance Gymnastics Academy, wanted to wait until all the competition seasons were over to move up kids and change workout schedules. The optionals season (Levels 6-10) is over now that it's May. We are starting our first official Level 4 workout.

If we learn all the required Level 4 skills, we get to compete Level 4 in the fall.

"When you get your kip you can use the cubbies upstairs," James says to us and disappears back into the offices.

"Marissa, do you know what he's talking about?" Savannah asks me.

"No," I say, "I've never noticed special cubbies before."

"Do we have time to check it out?" Trista asks.

"Technically, we have 3 minutes before class starts, we can run up and look," Paige says.

We run over to the stairs and head up to the second floor of PBGA. At the top of the stairs the dance studio is on the right, the parent viewing area to the front and left of us, and along the entire back wall of the parent viewing there are cubbies. They are similar to the cubbies down stairs, only there are names on each one. We walk over and see that small items are left in the cubbies like grips, tape, hair rubber bands, and a lot of them have notebooks decorated with pictures of famous gymnasts.

"Wow," Trista sighs, "this is cool. Their own cubby to leave stuff here."

"Kip Club," Savannah reads. I look up, above the cubbies are the words *Kip Club*.

"All these girls can do their kip?" I ask.

"Looks like it," Paige says, "guess that means we need to get work."

"Hey, you guys, look over here," we hear Trista say from the far left wall. She is standing in front of brown double doors that say *Optionals Study Room* across both doors in bright pink and black letters. "What do you think is in here?"

We walk over to her and stand in front of it for a moment. Trista looks at Paige and Paige shrugs. Trista pushes one of the doors open and we see Kayla sitting at a desk with a math book in front of her. Kayla is a Level 8 that we like to watch during practice. She is looks up as we peek in.

"Hi," she says. It's awkward for a second before she says, "Come in."

We timidly walk in and look around. On the far wall there's a window looking outside. On the side walls there are lockers with names on them. Along the wall closest to us there are three desks with lamps. The middle desk has a computer on it. In the center of the room there is an area rug with fluffy chairs and bean bags positioned in a circle around a coffee table.

"What is this place?" Trista asks.

"It's a study room for the Optional Team," Kayla answers. We look at her blankly, so she continues, "We are here so many hours that Katie made us a study room. Like today, I don't have time to go home before practice, so I come straight here and get a little homework done before workout," she explains.

"Do you guys hang out here too? It looks fun," Savannah asks.

"Sometimes, especially on Friday and Saturday when we don't have to rush home," she answers.

"How many hours do you train?" I ask her.

"Well, I'm a Level 8, so I train 19 hours a week. But the Level 9s and 10s are here 24 hours a week."

"Wow," Trista sighs, "Are you here every day?"

"Five days a week," she says. "What Level are you guys? Level 3?"

"We're new Level 4s," I answer.

"Well, good luck with that kip," she says with a smile.

"Is it really that hard?" Trista asks.

"For me it was, some kids get it faster. But it's the first skill that ever gave me serious trouble," she admits. I can't imagine Kayla having trouble with a kip, I see her doing them all the time in practice.

"We better get back; our three minutes are up. James will be wondering what happened to us," Paige says.

"Bye guys, see you down there in a bit," Kayla says and turns back to her math book.

As soon as we are out the door Trista is gushing about how cool it is that they have their own room. We walk past the Kip Club cubbies and down the stairs. Thankfully James hasn't emerged from the offices yet and we hurry out into the gym because now we're late. We walk over to the empty uneven bars and start practicing kips on the low bar.

There are two sets of bars next to each other. Trista, Paige, and Savannah take one set and Alexis and I take another set. Two people take a turn on the low bar while the others wait on the panel mat ready to go as soon as there is space on the bar. James has taught us to go one after the other without wasting time in between.

"Hi guys," Carmen says bouncing up to us. "James said to join you on kips."

"You're a Level 4 now?" Alexis asks. Carmen didn't compete Level 3 with us, but she has been working out with us since out competition season ended.

"I'm going to train with you guys this spring and summer and see if I can skip Level 3," she explains.

"Join our bar," Alexis says and I move over and make room for Carmen on the panel mat. Alexis jumps to the bar, glides her feet out, pulls her toes to the bar, and swings up into a support position. But before she gets to a support position on the bar she falls, not making the kip.

That's how we're all doing it. Gilde, toes to the bar, swing up, and before we can make it to a support position we fall back down to our feet. I watch my teammates try kips over and over. None of us make it.

But we will, we always do. We always learn the new skills for the next level. And this summer we will all learn the Level 4 skills and be an awesome team in September!

About the Author

Melisa Torres grew up in San Jose, California. She trained at Almaden Valley Gymnastics Club where she competed in USA Gymnastics' Junior Olympic program for ten years. Melisa then went to compete for Utah State University where she was a two-time Academic All-American and team captain.

Melisa currently lives in Utah and is a single mother to two active boys. Their favorite things to do together are skiing, swimming, going to the library, and dancing in the kitchen.

Read all the books in the
Perfect Balance Gymnastics Series!

PERFECT BALANCE GYMNASTICS SERIES

Grace and Confidence for Life!

MELISATORRES.COM
*For unique gymnastics gifts,
Book signing dates, and to apply for our
Reader of the Month Program.*

FACEBOOK.COM/PBGSERIES
*For articles about gymnastics and
updates on new releases.*

@PERFECTBALANCEGYMBOOKS
*Following gymnasts and young writers to
give encouragement and inspiration*

Made in the USA
Monee, IL
05 October 2021